MW00415023

Clint Hurley and his faithf
Dog, Josie, save a runaway girl from drowning, on a snowy Christmas Day. Now he is faced with a choice. Should he turn her over to the authorities or "rescue" her from far more than the river?

I continue moving and Josie is down the bank racing toward the river. My heart is pounding at the uncertainty of this. I negotiate the bank cautiously. She is at the water's edge and barking continuously. The last flicker of sun is enough for me to see that the yellow kayak, moving our way, contains a small child. The kayak will be past us in just a moment as the steady current is moving it along at a firm pace. A runaway child, in a kayak on the river, on a snowy Christmas Day. This is like a scene from a movie but there is no Matt Damon to rescue her. There is only an old man and a young dog. As I am contemplating what to do the situation turns brusquely grave. She leans too far to one side and the kayak capsizes. She is struggling to stay above water as the kayak is carried away with the current.

Praise for Billy Beasley's novel, The Preacher's Letter"

A GREAT, really good read. You did it again Billy. Stayed up till dawn reading it. They should come with a warning label, may cause lack of sleep!"—***Pat Bradford, Editor, Publisher, Wrightsville Beach Magazine***

Praise for The Girl in the River

"***I don't think*** I've ever had a first chapter in a book hit me that hard. Now I'm dying to see where it goes from here! If the rest of this book is this good I need to start on it early one morning because I doubt I'll be able to put it down."—***Herman Dickens, Avid reader***

"This author has the gift of keeping you on the edge of your seat with each line. I love how he incorporates the local flavor in his novels. It makes you feel as if you can walk outside and enter the story, yourself. Anyone who reads his first book, will be hooked and follow suit with the others, eagerly awaiting each one to be released!"—*Kevin Keen, Avid reader*

"Prepare to be immersed in the surroundings and characters as you read this book. You will feel a variety of emotions as you walk this journey with the characters that quickly, feel like close friends. You will not want to put it down, but you will not want it to end."—*Kristy Huddle, Acquisitions editor, Comfort Publishing*

"Heartwarming stories don't come any better than the ones that are penned by Billy Beasley".—*Sue Pearce, Avid reader*

"Once again, Billy Beasley has upheld his reputation as an amazing storyteller, with *The Girl in the River*. The voice of his character, Clint, is like a conversation with a wise and trusted friend. Another incredible story."—*Mary Ellen Poole, Avid reader*

"This was an enjoyable read. I felt a connection to each character. Each paragraph left me anxious to read the next."—*Cynthia Chapman, Retired music teacher*

"I can't wait to read this "book! I have read this author's other books and could not put them down!!The characters all seem so real and raw and true! The story line grabs your attention and keeps you riveted."—*Karen Kapusta, Lifepoint Church*

"Your first book, The River Hideaway, was one of two of my all-time favorites. The Girl in The River may even be my all-time number one favorite of all the books I have read. Such real-life characters and an intriguing story line make this book impossible to put down."—*Linda Brown*

"Billy Beasley has become my favorite author. His first novel, The River Hideaway, should be made into a movie.

It is that good.   I just read the opening chapter of The Girl In The River. The characters captivated me from the first sentence and I literally had tears in my eyes. I will pull an all nighter when this book is finally in my hands."—*Wylene Booth McDonald, Retired Merck & Company*

"Billy's ability to set a scene that has you seeing the story while you read is incredible. The story immediately draws you in and the characters are developed in a way that you feel you've known them for years... *The Girl in the River* ...will be hard to put down, and will be remembered long after the last page is read."—*Katie Olivolo, Former professor, UNCW & Coastal Carolina*

"The mark of a great book is being drawn into the story from the very first few pages....I was thoroughly engaged on a very human emotional level. Can't wait to see where this goes."—*Jayne Malach, Retired Librarian*

"The Girl in the River is a definite page turner that captures your attention early and holds it throughout the whole book. I've read everything Billy Beasley has written and this is his finest piece thus far."—*Todd Osborne, Avid reader*

"Billy Beasley's knack for writing about real-life issues that invoke an emotional bond with his characters creates a hunger for the next chapter...his first, *The River Hideaway* was so mesmerizing it would play well on the big screen."— *Debbie Neal, Avid reader*

"Having read the first five sample pages, I can't wait to see where this story goes. The main character is appropriately world weary and the love interest is intriguing. A good start that leaves the reader wanting more."—*Joseph McSpadden, Host of the Village Night Owl Podcast and Contributing Editor, Okra magazine*

For My Girls

Other Works

The River Hideaway, novel, released April 27, 2014

The Preacher's Letter, novel, released January 9, 2018

Currently write a monthly column for *Mustard Seed Sentinel Magazine*

Article published in *Optimist International* Magazine, Summer 2016

THE GIRL IN THE RIVER

Billy Beasley

Moonshine Cove Publishing, LLC

Abbeville, South Carolina U.S.A.
First Moonshine Cove Edition July 2020

ISBN: 978-1-945181-870
Library of Congress PCN: 2020911611
© Copyright 2020 by Billy Beasley

This book is a work of fiction. Names, characters, places and incidents are products of the author's imagination or are used fictitiously. Any resemblance to actual events, locales or persons, living or dead, is entirely coincidental.

All rights reserved. No part of this book may be reproduced in whole or in part without written permission from the publisher except by reviewers who may quote brief excerpts in connection with a review in a newspaper, magazine or electronic publication; nor may any part of this book be reproduced, stored in a retrieval system or transmitted in any form or by any means electronic, mechanical, photocopying, recording or any other means, without written permission from the publisher.

Cover photographs public domain; cover and interior design by Moonshine Cove staff

About the Author

It was 1998 when Billy Beasley, while watching one of his favorite movies, *A Time to Kill,* had a thought. What if a rich white kid and a black kid, met on a basketball court in the sixties and became best friends. And that friendship would ultimately be tested by the racially charged times.

Billy was determined to be published traditionally and weathered many rejections along the way. It was in 2013, when his new wife, asked when was the last time he had tried to get published. It had been a few years. He randomly selected one publisher and sent the story out to appease her. Later that year, he was offered a contract for *The River Hideaway.* The story he began in 1998.

The Preacher's Letter, his second published novel, was released in January of 2018.

He wrote an article about his old baseball coach, who he credits with being that one person, who long ago, turned a wayward young man's life around. The article was published in *Optimist International Magazine* Summer 2016.

Always more engaged to write stories than to tackle the arduous task of finding a publisher to say yes. There are completed stories resting in his computer today that he hopes to see in print one day.

Billy resides in Carolina Beach, North Carolina, with his beautiful wife and biggest supporter, Julie, and their Australian Cattle Dog, Teke.

www.billybeasley.com

Acknowledgments

My son, Micah, who has been with me for the entire journey.

My childhood friend, Nicky. I hope you would approve of the character I created in your memory. Words can't convey how much I miss your friendship.

All the kids who once called me 'Coach' and especially to the men that still do.

Kristy Huddle.

Gene Robinson and the staff of Moonshine Cove Publishing.

THE GIRL IN
THE RIVER

Part I
One
Clint
Thanksgiving

The first light of day leaked through the hospital window. I moved to close the blinds more securely in hopes that she will continue to rest.

"Please let the light in, Baby." She still calls me 'Baby' despite the fact that I turned seventy-two earlier this month. I move to her and she manages a slight smile but it's her emerald eyes that always seem to drink me in as if I'm better looking than a young Paul Newman. Trust me. I am far from it.

Allie has wielded such an influence over me since we first met over thirty years ago. Most of the time she's happy with me, though when I hear my name, 'Clint Hurley,' as opposed to just Clint, I know she's perturbed with me, but it never lingers.

We both survived failed starter marriages—brought about by marrying too early in life. I always believed that the divorce rate could be sliced in half if people waited until they were at least thirty years of age to wed. Certainly, that should at the very least be the case for men because we mature slower and we never really catch up with the women in our lives.

I was forty years of age when we married. Allie was twenty-eight. I still don't know why she wanted me. I was damaged goods, worn down by life, when she sought me out one day across the church parking lot on a miserable, gray, January day. My plan at that moment was to drive home to Carolina Beach, where a crock pot of white chicken chili, cold Molson Beer, and an afternoon of viewing football awaited me.

I had one hand on the door handle of my beaten up '68 Chevrolet Truck when I saw her walking in my direction with purpose. She was young, gorgeous and I turned to see where she was heading.

I turned back and she was grinning broadly. "No, it's you I want." She laughed loudly, without embarrassment or regret, when she realized how her statement sounded. "I mean I would like to take you to lunch."

There were times in my life I had been really smooth with women. That day was not one of them. "Why?" I asked incredulously. She said later that there was a look of bewilderment etched upon my face.

"Why not?"

And then it struck me what her motives surely must be. "Aw," I said. Surely, you are amazed by now as to my stunning conversational skills. I would like to inform you that I'm a lot better now, but that would not be accurate.

She once asked how a man could talk so much in his profession as a high school basketball coach and barely muster five sentences at home. I responded by saying that I had her to do my talking away from basketball. She turned her head to the side and looked at me sternly but I knew she was not upset. You spend the better part of a lifetime with someone and you learn their every expression. This look, I knew to be one of amusement.

"It's not about seeking out lonely people as the minister stated ten minutes ago."

I hate it when you think you have ascertained what is transpiring only to be left dumbstruck because your theory is erroneous. I stood frozen trying to comprehend why this lady with such an authentic grin that there should be songs written about it desired to take the likes of someone like me to lunch.

"Does scrunching your face, tightening your eyes, and turning your head slightly to the left help you understand things better?" She asked this as if she truly wanted to know.

I was unable to form a response. Beautiful lady wants to take me out to lunch but I was so sure that she was not interested in me that right then the chili, beer, and football seemed the better option. Her hair was long, wavy and the color of chestnut. She was wearing a long sleeve, brown and white dress that's two inches above her knee, her body is toned and shapely and I suppose that I shouldn't have been eyeing her legs in the church parking lot but I did. It has been a long time since I have been in close quarters with a woman. The last relationship, if you could call it that, has been over for two years. She broke it off because she didn't think that I was going to marry her. She was correct. I had no plans to ever marry again. The first one that took place in my twenties would make my current Sunday afternoon plans seem like a trip to the Caribbean Islands with the latest *Sports Illustrated* swimsuit model, on the most frigid, gloomy day of winter.

"You mean meet somewhere for lunch?" There, I had discovered my voice.

She opened my passenger door and said, "I'll ride with you if that's okay?"

It didn't seem to be much of a question. She was inside my truck now that had not witnessed a thorough cleaning since the Nixon administration.

I opened the door and said dryly, "And the last anyone ever heard of that silly young woman was that she foolishly got into some strange man's truck in the church parking lot. They still have not located all of her body parts." She giggled. "I checked your references. I know I'm safe. You want to know what I discovered about you?"

Slowly, I shook my head no.

It failed to dissuade her. "You don't allow but a select few people to get close to you, but those that you allow inside—there's no limit to your loyalty and protection." She paused before adding, "I knew I was safe with you without hearing any of that."

I drove to a non-descript family style restaurant in the Monkey Junction area that has been closed now for decades. The name of the place escapes me. It was typical of many of the southern family restaurants of that period, in Wilmington, North Carolina. Pick a meat and three sides, biscuits slathered in butter, along with a huge glass of sweet tea that would be refilled multiple times.

I could not believe a woman so fit could eat so much, but she ate all the food on her plate, and began nibbling from mine like we had been dining together for years.

She spoke easily about her life. She married her high school sweetheart the day after graduation. They were married for five discontented years. She discovered he slept with a coworker. She packed her belongings, walked out, and never looked back.

Since then she dated occasionally but never found the one man who could make her laugh or smile just by the mere thought of him. She previously married on auto pilot was how she put it. She would not repeat that mistake.

"What keeps you up at night?"

Where did that question derive from? I shook my head slightly, not wanting to reply, but at least this one was easy to answer. "Two years ago, my team lost the State Championship in triple overtime. We were up by one point when a kid on the other team made a half-court shot at the buzzer. The ball hit the back of the rim and went straight up for ten feet, before falling through the net."

She nodded her limited understanding, while admitting she knew and cared nothing about sports.

At least she didn't attempt to console me as everyone else did and say that we would return to the finals one day and win. We never did. I coached another twenty-seven years at the same high school but we never made it that far again. That was my best team, our best chance, and some kid who I discovered later died of a heroin overdose, made a shot he could never equal in a million years. Of course, I have moved on from that night. Isn't that readily apparent? Here is a little secret for those of you who have never coached. You pick out any coach—regardless of the success they have enjoyed. They could have won twenty championships and they will tell you that it's the one or two heartbreaking losses that invade their sleep at night.

We left the restaurant that day and she suggested we take a walk after all the food we consumed. I started to point out that I really didn't eat as much as she did but by age forty you learn that talking about the amount of food a woman has eaten is probably not the best course of action.

I drove to Carolina Beach State Park and we walked for over an hour through the woods. Little did I know it at the time but that was the first of many hikes in the woods we would take through the years. It was one of her favorite things, though she drew the line at walking in the woods during the hot, humid months that our region so generously offers. The May flies and the no-see-ums ate you early and when the thunderstorms of summer left standing water, the mosquitoes attacked relentlessly.

We were standing on Sugarloaf Dune, looking out at the Cape Fear River. The dune is sixty feet above sea level on the island known as Pleasure Island, which consists of the towns of Carolina and Kure Beach.

It was named Sugarloaf by the early settlers who thought that from a distance it appeared to be a huge mound of sugar. History records that Native Americans gathered oysters and clams near the dune. Confederate soldiers camped on it during the Civil War.

We both spotted the Owl in a tree between the dune and the river. I felt like the character from the Wise Potato Chips Bag was staring back at us. "Isn't seeing an owl in the day time bad luck?"

Her smile faded for the first time. "We just left church. I believe in God, not superstition."

It was apparent at that moment she was ahead of me on spiritual matters just as she proved to be about nearly everything. It was okay. I learned early on that lagging behind her was as prized a place as I could possibly be.

We stood beside each other gazing out at the scenery. We could see Brunswick County on the other side. A majestic hawk soared over the water. I felt her hand intertwine in mine in the most natural of ways. I know this will be difficult to believe and I can't blame anyone who will say it's too cliché, but at that moment what I heard in my soul was that wonderfully, slow, poignant song, *Time in a Bottle,* by Jim Croce.

I had proven to be slow throughout the entire afternoon, so maybe I even shocked myself when I gently turned her to me and kissed her lightly and longingly. She cupped my face in her hands. "Thank you. That was nice." She unexpectedly laughed out loud. "Good thing I had some mints in my purse or our first kiss might be remembered as the taste of the southern diner we had lunch at."

"It was just a first kiss?"

"I certainly hope so," she answered with a smile so delicate and such a soothingly look in her eyes that it felt as if my heart skipped a beat.

I grasped her hand and took a step back. She told me later she would recall how I never blinked as I stared intently into her eyes. "I don't have much to offer. I teach History and I coach basketball and I have no ambition to do anything beyond that. You're younger and certainly prettier. I'm sure in a church the size of the one we attend that there are many younger, better suitors than a damaged man such as myself."

It would be the first time she ever said both of my names together. "Clint Hurley, you listen to me and you listen good. I have a feeling about us. But there's one thing you can't do." She paused as I waited for her to continue. Her eyes held a slight sadness and her smile had faded for the first time that afternoon. "I simply will not abide by you speaking despairingly about yourself. If you'll do this for me, I in return will *never* allow anyone to speak negatively of you."

She was good to her word even when her parents disapproved of her choice in a husband and made that clear on many occasions. It reached a breaking point during the first year of our marriage when she informed them they were no longer welcome in our home if they continued to speak ill of her husband. They grudgingly accepted her decision but the three of us were always like awkward strangers with each other right up until they died in an automobile wreck twelve years after I married their only child.

"And another thing." That would be a running joke in years to come. She always had another thing. We use to take trips to the mountains. Six hours in an automobile and she would talk ninety per cent of the time. I was okay with that. It was especially convenient when we attended a function together. I once coached a game in front of twelve thousand people and I was comfortable. But place me at a party of twenty people that I don't know well and I am as introverted a man as you'll find and I'll be looking longingly at all of the exits. I guess that doesn't make sense to most people.

I looked back at the hospital bed. My trip down memory lane stalled for a moment. Her eyes were closed and I perceived an ever so slight snore. I think of her hobby of buying old discarded items and refurbishing them into a work of art. She was shaping things from wood pallets long before it was trendy. Maybe that day on Sugarloaf I was another project. I'm praying that she has more time remaining to continue to remodel me. I really don't mind and Lord knows I still need a lot of improving.

Another of her passions is animals, particularly dogs. She has rescued at least a dozen dogs and brought them home in our years together. Many would say she rescued me as well and I have no disagreement with that statement.

Still, if I voiced either one of these reflections to her, I'm pretty certain that I would hear both my names called out.

Currently, there are no rescue dogs in our home at Carolina Beach, North Carolina. Well, maybe that's not entirely true. We have an Australian Cattle Dog. She always brought home little dogs that carried a good portion of Chihuahua in their genetic makeup. The most recent one, Sydny died three years ago.

My friend of many years, Bryan Daughtry, lives in Ohio. He is an avid outdoorsman and as part of that he very selectively breeds hunting dogs. Labrador Retrievers and German Shorthaired Pointers. He and his wife, Brie, retired several years ago and bought a small farm and delved into the cattle business. He discovered quickly that he needed dogs that would herd and that led to his breeding a few choice litters of Cattle Dogs.

He called one day last year and told me someone had returned one of his dogs. She was six months old. He said he just felt like I needed her, which was a strange thing for him to say. He asked if I wanted her. As all things were with Bryan, she came without charge. He's as generous a man as I have ever known.

Allie knew that I had always wanted one of his Labrador Retrievers. She preferred small dogs that she could cuddle with and besides she was the one who had to care for them as teaching and coaching kept me away from home so much, until I retired.

Allie's gaze met mine and read my silent question. She nodded her approval. She never denied me anything. And in my mind, I could never give her enough. Some people have said they were encouraged by our marriage—our love affair. I really don't know what to draw from that. It's not as if it were a great deal of work. We loved each other freely and it was important that we be happy with one another.

I was wondering how we were going to coordinate picking up our latest addition to the family. Another thing about my friend Bryan—he's always one step ahead. The next words we heard were. "My annual hunting trip to West Virginia is two weeks from today.

We'll settle in there and when it's a good time for a break, we'll drive her to you."

"You don't…" my wife began. I held my hand up and shook my head slightly knowing that you never will talk Bryan out of anything he wants to do for you.

"Allie, do you still look at my friend like he's the only man alive?"

She chuckled softly. "I suppose I do."

"That's all I ever will ask of you. I never saw him light up around anyone like he did until you walked into his life. You take care of my friend. That's all the payment required."

Bryan has felt that way about her from the first time he met her. Allie has a spirit so true—so genuine that unless you're completely dense you can't help but be drawn into the exquisiteness of her grace.

"Bryan, you said we. I assume Ben will be with you on the trip?" Allie inquired. Ben is Bryan's son and has followed in his dad's footsteps as an outdoorsman.

"Yes ma'am."

"Maybe Ben and you could stay for dinner and spend the night when you bring her?"

"Now that, pretty lady we can certainly do."

"Also, we can call your cousin Patty and invite her to join us for dinner."

"That would be great."

I met Bryan years ago at a small fitness place in Wrightsville Beach. Our friendship has remained through the many peaks and valleys of our lives. We have lost touch at times, particularly living so far away from each other, but as we age, that's less likely to occur. Time has a way of teaching us all what is truly important.

I put my phone away, excited that I was finally getting a Labrador Retriever. I didn't know the color and I didn't care.

***

I was asleep in my recliner when Bryan and Ben arrived. I must have really been in a deep slumber because I heard the door open quietly but I heard no voices and I assumed it was Allie. Quickly, I fell back asleep. I woke with a puppy laying her neck across mine. Imagine my surprise when I raised my head to look at her and I saw a Red Heeler with one big red patch that consumed her right eye. My Labrador Retriever was an Australian Cattle Dog.

I would learn that laying her neck on mine was her love language. At night, she has always slept between us. If I turn away from her, she often rises up and places her neck strongly on mine. She won't budge until I turn back to face her and then she quickly falls back asleep.

I have never had a dog that desired to be physically touching me as much as she does. My wife relishes the love she offers her but she knew from day one this dog, unlike the dogs before, would prove to be my dog.

Looking at Bryan, I said, "I thought I was getting a Lab. You tricked me."

"Guilty as charged." My big friend with the strong jaw, close cut black and gray hair and kind dark eyes said, "You want me to take her back?"

Her face was now hidden in my rib area. I shook my head no. "I figure you had a reason."

Ben cleared his throat and I smiled as I looked at him. I still see him as the little boy I met long ago but he's a fine young man, now in his thirties with his own family.

"Mr. Clint." Now that cracks me up that he still refers to me in that manner but there has always been a quiet politeness about him. "I had a dream. I saw her nuzzling you neck to neck and I told Dad."

My body chilled instantly. I shook my head and looked at Bryan." Why did they return her?"

"They didn't." I waited for him to explain.

"Ben told me about the dream. Initially, I wrote it off as just a silly dream with no meaning but it was two days later and I could not get it out of my mind. I drove to the farm two hours away where she was living. It was a cold day, snowing on and off. I found her outside the barn. She was shivering violently." He shook his head and I saw the anger build in his eyes. "I picked her up and took her to my truck. I always have some towels in the back, I dried her and then I wrapped her in my coat. We sat there with the engine idling and allowing the heat to slowly warm her. She finally stopped shaking and I gave her some water from a bottle I had. She drank it hurriedly. I got some dog food and a bowl from a storage container I keep in the truck. She ate so fast that I had to take it from her and feed her out of my hand, a little bit at a time. I didn't want her to eat so fast that she got sick."

He breathed in deeply. "I sat there and I knew I should just drive away but my anger got the best of me. I may be in my sixties but you hurt a dog or a child in my sight and I'll take you out.

"About then the previous owner drove up. I got out of my truck to meet him.

"The man looked puzzled to see me. He offered to shake my hand and I refused. You left the dog outside in this weather with no water or anything?"

He shrugged and said, "Dog has to be tough to herd cattle."

Bryan continued, "She could die under these conditions and when was the last time you fed her? Have you taken her to the vet for checkups or do you even have a vet for her?

"He offered that he would do better and I told him he was not killing my dog with his negligence and stupidity. I might not have used those exact words.

"He said it was his dog and then he attempted to open my truck door. She started whimpering and backing up into the corner. She peed on my seat because she was so afraid. I put one hand on his shoulder and turned him toward me and I hit him with my other. He slid down the truck door.

"He mumbled something about eight hundred dollars he had paid for her. I dragged him out of the way of my truck and gave him one thousand dollars and insisted he sign a contract, stating that he was returning her to me. He complied."

It was quiet then, well except for some sniffles from my tenderhearted wife, who was now beside me and rubbing our new addition. She lifted her face to Allie who began kissing her nose.

"Does she have a name?" Allie asked.

"Josie."

"Josie?" Somehow, I could not picture the man he had just described as naming her that.

Bryan shook his head once again. "Tell him, Ben."

"You called her Josie in the dream, so we named her that. I don't think that idiot had even given her a name."

***

Josie is home while I'm at the hospital with Allie. I'm sure she's wondering where we are. Thankfully, we have a good neighbor, Sharon, who when Allie first entered the hospital asked for a key to our house and told me not to worry one moment about Josie. Sharon has been more than true to her word.

Allie patted the bed gently with her left arm. "What are you thinking about?" I took her hand and sat cautiously on the bed, making certain to avoid the IV drip inserted in her arm.

I tried my best to smile and not let her see the apprehension that engulfs me. "I was thinking about Josie and how much she misses you."

"Now, we both know Josie is your dog. You were right all those years ago when I kept bringing little dogs home and you said that I would love a Lab just as much. But Bryan pulled a fast one and we got ourselves a cattle dog." She laughed softly.

"But the first time I put her down on the floor after Bryan and Ben delivered her, she walked straight to the kitchen and nuzzled you. She knew who the boss was."

"I was cooking and she knew where the food was."

Without warning, Allie became ill twelve weeks ago and she has lost thirty pounds. Doctors have come and gone. There have been multiple trips to Duke Hospital. I long ago lost count of how many different tests have been run. Finally, they discovered a brain tumor. We can opt for a very risky surgery; even if she survived the operation. There's a very good chance that she would be in a state of knowing no one, her memory erased. She refused to risk losing our lifetime of cherished memories over a surgery that was as risky as deciding to kayak in hurricane. Chemo has yet to make a dent in the tumor and in each of the last three scans the tumor has grown.

She grasped my hand firmly and our gaze locked into one another. Her hair is gray and shoulder length. She has skin that belongs on a much younger woman but the centerpiece is her eyes. They look like the nearby Atlantic Ocean on one of those days that it's a vivid shade of green and you can see the floor of the sea when you're in the water up to your shoulders. I realize to the rest of the world she probably looks haggard but I only see my beautiful wife.

"Take me home."

I was stunned by her request, and it shows as I am unable to speak. It means that she has lost hope and without her what hope do I possess? We both live our life of faith together but hers is always stronger. I thought with the age difference I would go first and I selfishly desired it to be that way.

"You can do this," she said.

I shook my head in tiny shakes. "Don't give up."

"We both know this cancer is not letting go. I don't want to die here. I don't want any more chemo treatments. I want you to take me home. It's our time of year. Hallmark is playing Christmas movies nonstop. We still have time to create a few more memories."

Some requests in life are far more arduous to grant than others and this one topped the list in my life. I wanted to argue but knowing the depth of her spiritual life if she says this is her time, I concede that she's correct.

We have two sons, Wade and Dylan. They will not be pleased with me if I grant her wish. Somewhere along the journey my relationship with both has become strained. I really can't point to any incident that brought it about.

Wade and his wife Brittany live in Atlanta but he spends most of his time traveling all over the country purchasing land and creating mixed use developments. He has done well but he seems to have made the mistake of believing that the one with the most toys wins in the end. He's never content. One year he's collecting antique cars. The next he may sell them to buy sculptures. He and his wife seem to collect everything but cherished memories.

They decided not to have children because they didn't want anything to stop them from annual trips overseas or being able to travel on a moment's notice. Wade visited when his Mom became sick for the first time in three years. I recognize that I'm not much of a traveler but it's not as if he invites us to visit Atlanta. What would be the point? He would not be home anyway.

Brittany seems content with their life. I guess living in a four thousand square foot home in the suburbs of Atlanta—driving a Mercedes convertible, and being lavished with three hundred-dollar haircuts is enough to make her happy.

Our younger son, by two years, Dylan, lives in Columbia, South Carolina. He attended school at the University of South Carolina and met his wife Tara and never left. They own a plethora of commercial real estate. They did take a break from making money long enough to have two sons, James and Eric.

I always thought it would be great to have grandchildren but it can prove onerous when you seldom see them. James is ten years of age and Eric just turned eight. They are polite kids and my wife and I love them dearly, but I fear they are being raised by the nanny.

The great news is that we have two children that are multi-millionaires. The sad news is we don't have the closeness that we enjoyed when they grew up as simple beach kids.

Aside from teaching history and coaching basketball, I worked at various basketball clinics during the summers. Allie's main job was taking care of us, but she had a side business where she helped real estate agents by making the houses they were selling appear more inviting. Today, I believe it's called staging but when she began doing it, I'm not sure there was a term for it. We were never rich financially but we never hurt for anything.

She griped my hand once again. "Please take me home."

I nodded my agreement.

***

She died on a cold, clear Christmas Day as the sun faded that afternoon, leaving me in a place as dark, as the long winter night that blanketed the landscape.

Our sons and their families visited twice during that time. My sons didn't seem to want to spend time with their Mom, as much as they wanted to lecture me about removing her from the hospital. It didn't matter that I seldom left her and that hospice came each day. Our sons wanted her in the hospital. They wanted. They demanded. Children were not designed to be head of the families, especially ones as disengaged as our two sons. I have observed often in families that it's those that do the least that often possess the loudest voice and demand the most.

It reached the pinnacle the afternoon after her funeral service. Several friends and some of our church family were at our home.

The day was cool and crisp. The faultless sky was a vivid shade of rich blue. A brisk wind blew in from the Northeast. The front yard was nearly covered in dry leaves from the River Birch tree in front of our house and the neighbor's native Turkey Oak trees. My grandchildren were throwing a football in the yard with two neighborhood kids from across the cul-de-sac. You could hear the leaves crunch under their feet.

I stood on the porch watching them. Mainly, I was trying to escape the people inside the house. It would never feel like a home again without Allie. Standing there at that moment I came to a decision. I would sell the house and build our dream retirement home.

We purchased property in nearby Rocky Point years ago and the plan was that we would sell our home and build a modest log cabin. We planned to do as much of the work as we could. Allie, during her last week on this earth, suggested that I build the log cabin we had dreamed of building together. She knew I would never be able to remain in our home with decades of memories at every turn. I told her that I would consider it but it was hard to consider tomorrow when all I desired was to treasure every one of our last moments together.

Five years previous, we had a well dug and a sewer system installed. Our plan was to rent an RV and live in it while we built our cabin.

I thought about an old buddy and real estate agent, Bobby Brandon. I would call him in the morning and have him put the house on the market after the holidays.

Maybe it was my noticed absence in the house but people decided that it was time to depart. That included my sons and their families. People were filing out and giving me their best. So many people feel obligated to offer clichés that I have no time for. If one more person says to me, to stay strong—I may punch them in the throat.

Allie made me promise many things before she went to her final home. I was to keep attending church regularly. She also made me promise not to return to the disillusionment towards God that consumed me many years ago and was still prevalent when we met.

Christmas morning, before she slipped into unconsciousness never to return—she kissed me and said, "We will be together again. I'll have our home ready when you arrive." And then the last thing she said, I have no understanding of what it means.

Her eyes grew clear and it appeared as if her countenance returned temporarily to that of the young lady I married long ago. She smiled warmly. "Keep an eye out for your angel."

"What?" I asked, but she was gone.

"It's your fault," I heard our oldest son, Wade, say, in a loud, harsh voice, startling me from my thoughts. The people on the way to their cars were no doubt wishing that they were already in them and on their way far away from the impending conflict. Dylan stood beside him in support, though I doubted he would say anything. He has always deferred to his older brother.

"Do you have something on your mind?" I asked.

"You killed our Mom by taking her out of the hospital."

"Do you want to repeat that?"

"I said, old man, you killed our mom."

He looked at his brother, wearing a smirk that told me he was proud of his behavior. Seemingly without my knowledge, my right hand left my side and I hit him square in the face with a power I didn't know I still possessed. He fell into the dormant flower bed just off the porch. He lay there dazed as if he could not understand how he had come to find himself in such a precarious position.

It took him a while to gather himself and stand again. He started to speak and I silenced him with a look. I turned to Dylan. "Do you have anything clever to say to this 'old man'?"

He shook his head no.

"You boys go back to making money. It appears that is all you really have."

It was at this time I noticed that the Senior Pastor, Jeff was standing beside me. Maybe he thought I was going to hit someone else, but I was done and I carried no regret about what had transpired. I looked at him with unapologetic eyes.

He's in his forties and moved to Wilmington to plant a church that has grown so rapidly in twelve years that it's apparent it surprises even him.

"I think I would have decked him too," he said, before adding, "I'll see you in church." He gripped my shoulder firmly and walked away.

I stood there watching the cars depart. Dylan sat in their Cadillac Escalade with the engine idling, as they waited for the other vehicles to be out of the path of their escape route. I don't want you to think that he followed his brother in every decision. He bought a red Escalade as opposed to the black one that was behind him in the driveway that his brother's wife was driving. Wade's seat was laid back and he held a fancy silk teal handkerchief over his bleeding nose. There was a small part of me that began to regret striking him but the larger part thought a little humility might serve him well. Regardless, I doubt this was a story that he would regale his Country Club friends with.

The path was clear now. Dylan backed out of the drive. As the car came to a halt as he shifted to drive, I saw my grandsons seated in the back seat, look at me with confusion imprinted on their faces. Eric, the youngest waved slowly toward me. I wondered if I would ever see my grandchildren again.

I looked to the sky. "Look what a mess I've already made without you."

Everyone was gone. All that remained was Josie, myself, and my very limited supply of faith.

I walked into a house that I never thought could feel so desolate. The life had been sucked out of it. I removed a bottle of Crown Royal Whiskey from the back of the pantry. Allie and I both enjoyed an occasional drink by the fireplace on a cold winter night. I wanted to drain the entire bottle right now in hopes that it might numb the agony that raged inside me. I twisted the cap off and lifted the bottle to my lips.

The first swallow burned my throat, but then I paused, knowing it would disappoint her to see me reduced to this. I rested the cap back on the bottle and twisted it slowly until it came to a stop, and placed the bottle back in the pantry. I crumbled to the floor as my torrent of tears cascaded on to the pale gray ceramic tile.

I was curled up in a fetal position, when Josie laid her body on top of mine, her head burrowed under my neck. She whimpered softly. It was as if she was attempting to protect me from any injury that fell upon me from above, but the destruction that ravaged me derived from within.

Two
Clint
Thanksgiving Day (One year later)

Josie and I were relaxing inside the small log cabin that's now complete—save a few interior items that are not as vital as having a roof over our head and shelter from an unusually cold Thanksgiving Day. It's nearing one o'clock and I promised Josie a walk to the river this afternoon. She will be disenchanted if I don't follow through on my pledge.

The fire crackled and popped three times and Josie lifted her head and stared perplexed at the flames as if it were a living thing. She was situated comfortably on the rug I placed on the breve shaped stone tile in front of the fire place. The remainder of the flooring is a deep brown hardwood with the exceptions of the bathrooms and the laundry room that are done in concrete gray ceramic tile.

I sat in my worn but comfortable recliner. Allie would never have approved of my placing it directly in front of the fireplace. It would not be appropriate interior decorating that she so prided herself on.

It was not in its current position when Josie and I moved in, the first week in October. I moved it there the first time the night temperature dropped into the low forties. I was having another night of restless sleep. It was two a.m. when I built the first fire of the season. Josie watched with peaked curiosity but once the warmth of the fire reached her, she lay down in front of it and studied it for several minutes before joining me in my recliner.

She came to us with little or bad training, which is far worse than none at all. Bryan, as he was departing from our home the day after he delivered Josie, looked at Allie, and said, "If you baby this dog too much, she will run over you guys. You have to allow the old ball coach here a lot of leeway to be tough when the occasion calls for it. Look for a good trainer and check into an E-Collar. She's a working dog and she requires having her body and mind exercised. She's already behind in her training from my mistake of not better verifying the prior owner." His gaze moved to me. "You have to establish with her that you're the Alpha and she will not like it, but eventually she will respect that and you'll have a wonderful and loyal dog."

I did as Bryan instructed. Each morning I took her to Carolina Beach State Park. It's a wonderful Park, with several hundred acres of woods with well-maintained trails. During those first few months I would get so exasperated with her that I would throw down the leash and walk off in disgust. There were times that she stubbornly refused to move even as I walked twenty to thirty yards away from her. I would shake my head and mutter, "If she ever figures out that I'm not really going to leave her I'm in deep trouble." I never once had to go back to her on her terms. Eventually she gave in and would run toward me, her leash trailing behind her.

I also hired a wonderful trainer, Tom. He once was employed as a K9 officer with the Wilmington City Police. He still is an officer but his canine work these days consists of conducting training classes for others. He was as straight forward a trainer as I once was as a basketball coach. He had never trained a cattle dog before and I could tell right away he was intrigued. We met at the Park, where he conducted private training sessions with Josie and me.

I think he appreciated that I was coachable, even if for a long time Josie was not. He didn't suffer fools well and if the owners didn't want to follow through with his training methods he encouraged, no, rather he demanded they seek guidance elsewhere.

Despite his firmness and often gruff demeanor with Josie, she loved him. It brought to mind my coaching days when frequently the kid that you were the hardest on was the very one that loved you the most. Each day that she saw him she would break from me to run greet him. He would turn from her and pay her no mind until she did it the correct way, which was to return to me, and allow me to walk her on heel to him. Still, it was a battle to keep her from running to greet anyone that came near.

Allie insisted, even when she was sick, that I take Josie to the woods. I didn't want to leave her, even for a few minutes in the Park. She would tell me that she was weary of my company and she could use the break, but she never meant it. We never grew tired of spending time with each other.

The morning after Allie departed from this life, I spent time making all the arrangements. That afternoon with a house full of people and enough food to feed a family of fifty I excused myself to take Josie for our daily walk in the woods. Several people tried to dissuade me and some even offered to walk with me. I denied all their requests. Sometimes in this life, a man just needs time alone with his dog.

We hiked to Sugarloaf that day, where I sat on the wood bench, looked at the river and wept for several minutes. Josie curled in my lap and looked up toward me with a look of such great tenderness that it rivaled any that I have ever witnessed, in any form. The saddest of times was when I witnessed her walk from room to room in the house, searching for Allie. She would return to me with a look that seemed mixed with sorrow and a lack of comprehension.

Something seismically shifted in Josie's demeanor when we lost Allie. I trace it back to that afternoon when I left people in my house for quiet time with Josie. That day she followed my every request without hesitation, without the struggle of her wanting her way. Each time I gave the command, "Scout," which meant she was free to roam ahead, to smell and inquire into all the things her heightened senses compelled her to explore—she would hesitate and look at me with sad amber colored eyes and I would tell her that it was okay. She would scout several feet in front of me for a few seconds and then immediately return to walking by my side. She was on heel without a lead and I was lost in my grief, wondering how I could make it through this life for another day, for another minute, feeling as if the larger part of my heart had been viciously ripped away with no chance of restoration.

I walked in such a daze that I forgot to periodically look behind me for the occasional jogger, when a man, wearing a red NC State hoodie, with a big Wolfpack emblem on the back of it had already passed us and by the time my senses collected he was twenty yards in front of us. Josie showed no interest in greeting him, and I have had encounters in these woods, in which her greeting people, was not anything they were particularly excited about. I looked beside me and Josie kept matching my steps with no inclination to do otherwise. I knelt down and praised her softly and offered her one of the treats I always carried with me. She ignored the treat initially, looking at me as if to convey that staying with me required no reward. I kissed her snout and encouraged her to take the treat, which she took gingerly. From that time forward, it's as if she grew up and left being a puppy behind. Josie was a working dog and while there were no cattle to herd, she somehow knew that I was her job, and it was a task that was no job for her at all. It was her mission, her calling, to keep whom she loved the most, moving forward, however tentatively that proved at times.

Occasionally, I would find laughter in something. Maybe something someone said as we worked on the cabin. My spirit would lift, and I could tell that Josie had noticed by her sudden boost of energy and she would use this time to bark and dart toward me and then quickly sprint away in her own game of tag. Allie use to refer to this as her running fit and when she was a puppy Allie was often the one who would take her out back to our patio and let her run the energy off before bedtime. This was usually mandated by Josie standing on the couch and barking continuously at us as we tried to watch television. I would pin her at times and tell her to, "Settle." Sometimes it worked to a degree, but even as you were given her that firm command and she was calm, she still insisted on letting out one last muffled bark under her breath. I use to tell Allie that she was just like her. Always having to have the last word.

After moving the recliner several feet to its existing place, I constructed a small book shelf that rested beside the recliner, from some of the materials from the scrap wood pile. Allie would not approve of this either but she would endorse that on top of the book shelf was my Bible. I read a few passages each morning and then I pray. It's not as if God is not available anytime but it's the morning when my mind is the clearest and I am able to better focus.

The fire popped again and Josie woke and kissed me on my whiskered cheek. She lay still next to me for a few moments before changing her position, turning her head toward the fire, laying her head on my leg and politely sticking her behind on my chest. The fire cracked again and she growled at it. She raised her head and rendered a slightly exasperated snort.

"It's okay, sweet girl," I say, as I rub her back. There was a nearly dead large pear tree on a farm a half mile away from here and I garnered permission from the owner to cut it down. He was happy to be rid of it and he had no use for the firewood. He had become modernized and his fireplace was powered by propane just as the one was at our home in Carolina Beach. I know that gas fireplaces are efficient, neater, and far less trouble than gathering wood, but Allie and I always had our heart set on a wood fireplace.

It was last spring when I cut the tree into firewood for a time like the present when it would pay handsome dividends. I enjoy the occasional crackling and sizzling produced from the tree, even if Josie does not.

I immersed myself into building this cabin, toiling long arduous days, as if I were a much younger man. I lost ten pounds in the process but I don't know if that can be solely accredited to my labor. My appetite, though slightly better of late, was hit or miss for the first several months of this forlorn year. Nothing is the same without Allie. I long every day to cross over and be united with her once again.

The exhaustion I felt each day after working on the cabin enabled me to at least gain a few hours of sleep. Occasionally, I had two drinks of Crown Royal to aid my sleep. It was something my dad once did when he worked the night shift as a Police Dispatcher at Wrightsville Beach. It was kind of funny to survey him down two shots of Jim Beam at seven o'clock in the morning, considering the man never really drank. He rarely drank beer, except on the occasion, when his doctor advised him to when he was suffering with habitual kidney stones. I never saw him with a mixed drink. His only other use for whiskey was when he had a cold and he would make a hot toddy.

It's too bad he didn't show the same restraint with cigarettes, which led to his ultimate demise, in the form of lung cancer when he was sixty-two years old. Mom died one year later because life was too hard without him. I understand that now as I have struggled through this first year of life without my Allie.

I think Allie would favor the layout that I chose. We had planned to build a slightly larger version than the one I ultimately decided to construct. But with her gone, I chose an open layout with two nice sky lights to allow the light in that she craved. Most of the living quarters were downstairs but there was an upstairs loft and a bathroom. Maybe my grandsons would stay in the loft one day.

The downstairs contained a functional kitchen and dining area, along with two modest bedrooms and a small bathroom for each. The cabin was certainly unpretentious.

I know without question what her favorite aspect of the cabin would be. The front and back of the home have a porch the width of the house. The front porch is nice but I rarely sit there. The back one offers more privacy and I can see the sunset filter through the trees as it beds down over the Cape Fear River. I wish my Allie was here to sit in a rocker beside me and hold my hand as she so loved to do.

It's for certain that while Allie really liked log cabins—she also wanted this for me because she knew I loved the simplicity of a log cabin and especially fancied the ruggedness of having wood dominate it. There's not a piece of sheet rock in the entire fourteen hundred plus square feet.

Pastor Jeff, despite observing me knock my son on his behind, sent a team of volunteers to help me get started with the footings. He even made certain that the leader of the group, Foster, was present. Foster is a retired veteran of the Coast Guard who had also dabbled in selling log cabin kits in the area for a few years. Foster and his wife Carol constructed the log cabin that they presently live in, not more than five miles from mine.

It was a thoughtful gesture on Jeff's part and it led me to hire Foster. He worked for such modest wages that I felt as if I was taking advantage of him. I discussed this with him as I came to realize in a very short time, that he was quite skilled and not a laborer to be working for fifteen dollars per hour. He told me that he and his wife Carol had been blessed and highly favored and they didn't want for anything. I insulted him once when I added one hundred dollars to his weekly wages. He didn't notice the extra currency until he arrived home. He drove right back and knocked on the RV. He gave me the one-hundred-dollar bill and said he would work only for the wages agreed upon and if I tried to overpay him again, he would be forced to cease working with me. I apologized and we moved past by mistaken attempt at a good deed.

Paying him his proposed wage proved to be the best deal I ever received anywhere or anytime in my life. I would have been lost without him and I think that's why he wanted to work with me. Despite his considerable knowledge and my lack thereof, he always treated me as if I were in charge. He knew what to do but he always deferred to me. As he often stated, "It's after all, going to be the home you live in."

I still don't know if Foster is his first or last name. He's a quiet man who talks rarely—save when it was necessary for work. He's a few years younger than me and still has his hair cut in a military style. The majority of it's still black with only a few slight speckles of gray. He's very fit. He may be in his early sixties but the size of his chest and broad shoulders lends itself to a far younger man.

I also hired Trey, a brash talking man of twenty for help back in the late spring. He showed up one day and asked if I was hiring. I was in dire need of help and asked if he could begin the next day and he responded that he would be happy to begin right that minute, which he did.

He's a capable worker but like so many young men, he's rather enamored of himself and quite the chatterbox.

He told Foster one day that he bet he could do more pushups than he could. Foster kept working and ignored him for several days. The kid never allowing the subject to completely rest.

One day as the kid kept talking, I was about to tell him to pack his gear and seek his employment elsewhere. Foster sensed this and he gave me a tiny shake of his head.

"Okay, Trey," Foster said.

"What?" Trey asked, not sure which of his words landed, considering the plethora of ones he had so generously offered.

"Pushups."

Now Trey was excited. "How much? Twenty dollars?"

Foster shook his head. "I won't take your money."

"But..."

Foster held his hand up and the kid became quiet. "I'll stay late and do your cleanup each day for one month." Trey was responsible for cleaning and gathering tools and materials at the end of each day as Foster and I finished whatever task we were presently working on that day.

Trey's eyes perked up at the thought of that. "You're not going to win but what is the bet if you did?"

"You'll go to church with me each Sunday for one month. No excuses."

The kid was so confident that he readily agreed to the bet.

It was settled upon that I would count out loud.

The kid went first and I was surprised when he performed sixty pushups. Foster got into position on the floor and began to do pushups with such a fluid rhythm it seemed these were as easy for him as breathing.

"Fifty-seven, fifty-eight, fifty-nine, sixty," and he's still maintaining the same cadence he began with. "Sixty-one," I say. He stops and stands. Looking at a finally speechless young man he said, "Church begins at nine thirty and I'll meet you in the parking lot at nine fifteen."

I could tell by the non-committal nod and expression on his face that Trey is planning to weasel out of the wager. "Trey," I said, and he turned in my direction. "If you fail to honor your word at any of the next four Sundays, don't bother to show up here for work."

"You can't do that."

"Pretty sure I can."

"But..."

I took one step closer to him. He was so uncomfortable that he backed up. He had no worries. I am through hitting people. I pointed my finger at him. "You ran your mouth for days about this wager and every other subject under the sun. Don't you ever tire of the sound of your voice?"

He started to speak.

"No," I said, shaking my head. "That's a rhetorical question. Trey, I have no use for a man that does not keep his word. I'll be standing with Foster in the parking lot this Sunday and the ones to come. Are we clear?"

The kid actually said, "Yes, sir." I noticed Foster smile. Trey honored his bet and was even early each Sunday. At first you could tell he didn't want to be there when the worship began but over the next month he loosened up. The last Sunday that concluded the wager, Foster invited him home for Sunday dinner. Foster's wife, Carol took a liking to the young man who had no mother. She had abandoned him long ago and he was left to be raised by his father and three older brothers. It was not an easy life. He felt he constantly had to prove that he was as tough as they were. Miss Carol showed him a softer side, a mother's love, and he often visits with them and even after the bet was concluded, occasionally joined them at church. If I didn't know better, I would think that Foster had the entire thing planned.

Foster has a disarming slight smile much of the time. There's contentment about him that I have rarely found in any man. I have heard church members say he's as fine a Christian man as you'll find. I have also heard those same people add that he's the quietest man that they know as well. Frequently, as needs in the church community arise, he says nothing, but shows up to help take care of the problem. I believe his most cherished times are when he can complete the task alone without any fanfare or pats on the back. I know enough about him to know that he could care less about the praise of any man. He's the kind of man I once strived to be. I have come up woefully short.

The year has moved by painfully slow despite all the work that consumed much of my time. I have tried to do the things that Allie would have expected from me. I attended church most Sundays. The only uncomfortable part for me is that several of the older single women, especially the widows in the church have invited me to their homes for dinner. This began pretty much one month after Allie's departure. I guess one month of grieving was equal to thirty plus years of being with a woman that you knew to have no equal. I have no interest in dating or having someone to keep company with to fill the loneliness.

Allie and I both had Facebook pages. Three days after the funeral I shut hers down. It was nice all the wonderful things people posted but I could not bear it.

Women started using Facebook to contact me. Before Spring arrived, I deleted my page. Now, I don't want you to think that I am a bag of chips, and a butt load of hot sauce, as Allie use to say to me frequently. I was that to her but she had uncritical eyes. There are just a lot of lonesome people in the world that will do just about anything to not be alone.

The fire pops once more and Josie turns curiously toward me as if I can make it cease. She's a beautiful dog with the kindest eyes you can imagine. The hint of sadness exhibited in them I honestly think is because of her depth of feeling for me. I tap my stomach and she relocates her body in my lap, resting her head on my chest. She weighs thirty-eight pounds and that makes for an oversized lap dog but she finds a way to be comfortable. I began to rub her gently.

She lifts her head and looks at me. I rub her head softly and she lies back down and soon I perceive a slight snore. Praying silently, I thank God for helping me make it this far. He has not left me alone. How else do you explain that my realtor, Bobby, placed our home at Carolina Beach on the market the day after the New Year began and it was sold before the week was out? And I do mean sold. They paid with a certified check and had their attorney draw up all the paper work quickly. It helped that they didn't need a mortgage and I owed nothing on the house.

I didn't even have to rent an RV to live in during construction. Bobby had a friend who owed him a favor. The man owned a perfectly good RV that he had not used in two years. He graciously drove it here and hooked everything up and showed me the ins and outs of RV living.

Foster, Trey and I worked Monday through Friday each week, save the days we were rained out. Most Saturdays, I cut firewood and split it. I had three cords for the winter, which should be more than enough in the mild climate that makes up southeastern, North Carolina, but so far, this has been the coldest fall that I can recall.

I plan to heat the home primarily with the wood. It would hold down costs, but more importantly it would be yet another chore to keep me busy.

There's little in the way of family that remains, save my two sons and grandsons. I called earlier in the day and left messages at both homes but I don't expect to hear back from either son. I tried to make amends back in the Spring but when you're a man that holds himself in as high opinion as Wade does and you find yourself lying dazed on the ground, in front of several witnesses—suffice to say that's a difficult blow to recover from.

Not only are my parents gone but my two older brothers and one sister all died years ago. I was a late surprise gift for my parents.

None of my siblings remained in this area. My two brothers first left the area to work in the construction of military depots in Alaska before it was even granted state hood. Later they were among the first workers hired to work on the Alaska Pipeline. My sister married a military man and they spent most of his career stationed overseas. They loved Germany so much, where they spent the last few years of military life, that when he retired, they chose to reside there. My brothers never married. My sister and her husband could never have children.

Bryan visited in October once the cabin was livable to make sure I was still a worthy parent for Josie. He helped me for three days, assisting with the many tasks that were yet to be completed. He's one of the last real friends that I have remaining at this stage of life. Many have passed on and others moved away. It dawns on you one day that someone you once considered a dear friend you may have not spoken with in over a decade.

I am part of a large church and I know many people there. People that would drop everything and come to my aid if needed but when you only see these people in church related activities and never in a social setting, are they really friends or merely acquaintances? Don't get me wrong. I don't blame any of them. I certainly don't go out of my way to make friends. I go to church and enjoy the worship music, along with the poignant messages that Jeff offers. But when it's over, I don't exactly stick around to strike up conversation.

The plain truth is that I am content to live out my remaining years without adding new people into my life. My greatest hope is to reconcile with my sons and I pray for that every morning.

My phone played, *I can only Imagine,* by MercyMe. It's my favorite song. I speculate often as to how magnificent everything must be for Allie. It's easy to deliberate at this stage of life about the wonders of Heaven. I reflect as to if it's so perfect that Allie does not even miss me. I guess I'll have to find out the answer to that question when I join her.

Lost in thought, I answer the phone thinking it might be one of my sons. I should have checked the screen first.

It's Lori. She lives just down the road on the same long gravel road off Highway 210 that I do. She's sixty-three, blonde, petite, attractive and too nice. She has been widowed for five years and she has made no secret about her interest in me. But any interest is a one-way street, and she has not realized or accepted that it will remain so.

"Hello."

"Hey," she says in a voice brimming with cheer.

There's silence; if she's waiting for me to be forthcoming, she's in for a protracted wait.

"Are you there?"

"Yes."

"I was hoping that you might have changed your mind about coming for Thanksgiving dinner. My two sons and their families are here and we would love for you to join us."

"Thank you, Lori, but I'm fine."

There's silence and once again. I am not filling in the gaps.

"You don't have to be alone, you know. That's your choice."

"Yes, it is."

"I know you miss your wife…"

"Allie," I say firmly.

"Allie."

It's quiet again and I pray she might give up. I really don't want to be rude, but I have never suffered persistent people well.

"Look, I have been where you're at. You think you never want to move on, but…"

"Lori."

"Yes."

"Please do not be so bold as to tell me how I feel or how I'm going to feel in the future. Now, forgive my bluntness but I always believe the truth is best. You're a lovely woman but this situation is as dead as the dead-end road we live on. Please enjoy your Thanksgiving with your family. I'm content right where I am."

"Could I bring you some dinner over later?" You have to give her credit. She's not shy, nor does she lack determination.

"No, please don't bother with that. My friend Bryan brought me quite a bit of venison when he visited. I have a Crock-pot full of venison stew cooking right now." I already knew from a previous encounter that she hated trees being cut down, so surely, she would not approve of Bambi being served for dinner. I was about to be proven correct.

"You mean you eat deer?"

"Every chance I get."

"What about dessert?"

"Please enjoy the company of your family and don't bring any more food. I know you mean well but truthfully my appetite is not all that great these days, and food often goes to waste."

I think I just insulted her. I read the call ended words on my screen.

I don't know why but I chuckle about my dead-end road remark. Maybe it's because I live at the very end of the road.

This past June, Lori showed up for the first time, unannounced with enough food to feed a small army. I was in the process of removing the weaker of two trees that were less than a foot apart from each other. "I have some food I cooked for you." She paused and said, "You're not going to cut that beautiful tree down, are you?"

"Yes, and you need to move out the way. You can never tell if it might fall back toward you." Now, I knew that was a truth but this skinny oak tree that was no more than six inches in diameter was not falling back toward us. It was going to fall straight toward the river where I was directing it.

She started to speak and I motioned her back and then fired up the Stihl Chainsaw. I dropped the tree and cut the saw off. Hopefully, I could persuade her to leave quickly, so I could resume cutting up the remainder of the tree.

Maybe I'm somewhat cynical—okay, make that really cynical, but she was dressed in a colorful yellow sundress with deep blue patterns running through it. She wore open toed white sandals. I would like to think she's not dressed like this to impress me. But reverting back to my days as a basketball coach, I'll say this feels like a full court press.

"I have some food for you," she repeated. "I know it must be difficult to cook in that tiny RV while you work on your house." She looked to the house as if I would offer her a tour. The exterior of the house was complete and there was a good month's worth of work remaining inside.

"It's no problem," I stated as I pointed to the Weber Charcoal Grill.

She didn't know quite what to say to that. "Could I have a tour of your home?"

I smiled tightly. I was trying to be nice. I really was but she had her stylish sandals dug in and I don't think being overly nice would work. "There are too many things inside to trip you up right now." I hesitated and then added, "I don't want to be rude but I'm trying to gather enough firewood for next winter."

"You could just run the heat and save the trees," she offered.

"I could, but I won't."

I held my hands out for the food. The first thing I noticed is that it's all presented in a nice metal tray and none of the food is contained in paper plates and bowls. She's planning on coming back. Imagine her surprise when she discovered her kitchenware on her porch early the next morning, placed there before she woke.

Still, it has proven difficult to dissuade her. I bet she has made a dozen trips here since her initial visit and often armed with food. She also invited me to attend church with her. I informed her I was comfortable where I worshipped now. She told me to give her church a try and it was so much closer than driving so far into Wilmington. And so, it went.

Looking at the beautiful stone that surrounds the fireplace, my eyes drifted to the rough sawn beam that serves as the mantel. One picture stands out more than the others. It's our wedding day. Allie is holding me as I whisper in her ear. She has the most mischievous, sexy expression. I must have been saying something promising about the events to transpire that evening.

Allie posted the photo one day on Facebook. Jerry, an old adversary from my coaching days, remarked, "The caption should read would you buy a used car from this woman?"

I reminded Jerry once about his comment and he may have surpassed his initial quote, when he replied, "I mean no offense, but I would buy whatever Allie was selling."

I nudge Josie to get down and I slowly move out of the chair. I walk into the kitchen and lift the lid on the Crock-pot. It smells great and I cut the temperature back to warm. It will be fine like that for the rest of the day.

I walk back in the living room and turn the television on. There's always football on Thanksgiving Day. I did splurge and buy a sixty-inch television. Often in the middle of the night, I watch television until I can drift off to sleep.

Josie looks at me and walks to the back door. I don't move fast enough so she offers a muffled bark. What do you think that means? I grab the leash that hangs on a wooden peg by the back door and clip it to the ring on her teal collar.

We walk outside, greeted by the cold fall air. We enter the edge of the woods not far from the cabin and I unclip her leash. "Scout," I say to her and she takes off down the well-groomed path that winds through the forest toward the river.

We receive very little in the way of fall color here in the southeastern part of North Carolina and what we do enjoy arrives late in the year like now and into December. Most of the trees surrounding us are Oak and Pine trees, mixed in with Maples, Cherry and Sweetgum. The Oak trees I enjoy but I have never cared for Pine trees, except for the pine cones they produce that I use to start a fire with. I made sure any of them that were close enough to snap and fall on the cabin during a hurricane were cut down. I had that task done before construction began and the pulp wood company cut them down for the wood.

There's an occasional Dogwood tree growing in the woods and during a decent year where conditions are favorable, as they seem to be this season, their leaves change from green to scarlet, to a deep wine-crimson color.

There's one massive Hickory tree that offers bright yellow leaves so vivid that it reminds me of the times Allie and I drove on the Blue Ridge Parkway in October when the mountains became aglow with a spectacular array of color.

I walk past it and then turn back and look up and admire its majestic display. Josie ran ahead of me but very quietly she returned to sit by my left side. I chuckled softly and gave her a treat. "Good girl."

She was responding to something that I had taught her after being encouraged by Allie. We had fallen in love with the television show, *Heartland.* The pretty young blonde-haired lady would walk away from the horse and stop, and the horse in most cases would follow her and come to rest by her. I think the term she used was joining up. Josie was less than a year old when upon seeing that, Allie said, "You could teach her that." And today on a day I was merely stopping for a better vantage point to admire this glorious tree, Josie had performed what she had been taught. There was something about this trick that after coming to rest beside me she would look up at me with indulgent eyes.

Allie would often say, "Look at how she looks at you. She absolutely adores you."

I knelt and rubbed her head. She kissed me on the side of my face. I returned a kiss on top of her head. "Scout."

She took off toward the river. There's a vantage point to look across the river and we walk to that place as we do every day. Today we enjoy a sprinkling of yellow leaves from a clump of River Birches, located on the other side.

I stand and enjoy the fleeting peace that occurs on occasions such as this. Josie is sitting by my side. We observe two men, one in a yellow kayak and the other in a brown one that's almost lost in the murkiness of the river.

I shudder as I am cold enough just standing here. But they look well equipped for their excursion, judging by the apparel they are wearing. The man in the brown kayak raises his hand in greeting. I return the greeting, and then I look down at Josie. "I guess I didn't teach you how to wave."

Turning away from the river, I say to her, "Let's go back, sweet girl."

Three
Clint
Christmas Eve

It was eleven o'clock, Christmas Eve night. Christmas songs played on the truck radio. Josie sat in the passenger seat surveying the road.

I attended the last candlelight service at church tonight. No, Josie didn't go inside. The night is cool and she was happy to snuggle in the blanket I had for her that was laid out on the seat.

It was difficult to attend the service without Allie but I knew she would not want me to sit home alone on Christmas Eve. My one reservation was I didn't want invitations to Christmas Dinner and I was spared. Foster called earlier in the week and invited me to join his family, but all their kids and grandkids are in town and while I knew it was a sincere invitation, I would have felt lonelier in the presence of strangers than I would at the cabin with Josie. I have not heard from Lori since Thanksgiving. I hope I'm safe from any invitaion to be with her family.

Tonight, I was able to enjoy the ending when the lights were dimmed and all you could see were peaceful faces that glowed in candlelight, as "Silent Night" played. I held two candles this year. My Allie always with me in spirit and I do wish I could tell you that was enough but it's not, nor will it ever be. If God were to offer me a Christmas present this year it would be an easy choice. I would say take me home to my wife.

Thoughts like that remind me of the one constant in my life. What about Josie? I worried about what would happen to her for about ten seconds when I realized Bryan would undoubtedly take her right back to Ohio. I breathed heavily and reality set in. God is not going to grant my desire to go home to my girl. I'm probably here for several more years regardless of whether I care to be or not.

The positive is that despite the years I have remaining when the final trumpet sounds, I'll be home forever. I'll never have to worry about being separated from my Allie again. I know some people regard such faith and hope as utterly impractical and perhaps even foolish, but once you have truly experienced the love of God, there's little that can shake you from that belief.

Josie and I were headed toward Carolina Beach in my dark blue 1999 Chevy Silverado. It has a lot of miles on it, just like its owner. We were approaching Snow's Cut Bridge, the high bridge that transported you over the inlet below it. I remember often at the end of a work day the feeling of tranquility as you crossed over to Pleasure Island and left a far busier, less soothing world behind.

I drove through our old neighborhood and every single home was lit up with decorations. It was probably not a good idea to drive into the cul-de-sac that we once lived in but I did so anyway.

The new owners had strung lights in the Japanese Maple Trees that my sons and I planted together long ago. It's the only physical thing I miss from the house. I had not planted any at the cabin. It's hard at this stage of life to get excited about planting trees that are not exactly renowned for rapid growth. Besides, I have a forest all around me.

"Baby, I think I have done about as well as I could without you. I did something today that I know you would have been so pleased with me." I ceased speaking for a moment and I thought of how often she would look at me so endearingly and tell me she was proud of the man I was.

I never received those words from my parents, or anyone else for that matter. It meant the world to me, but then she was my world.

"The church was doing prep work today for the meals that will go out tomorrow. I volunteered. Pastor Jeff even insisted that I bring Josie inside. I instructed her to a place in a corner far from where we were set up and people were amazed that she laid there without moving for three hours, watching me intently the entire time.

"I'm lonely without you but I'm not depressed. I also have abided by your rule, no more than two drinks in any given day."

There was a time early in our lives together when I fell into the habit of having several drinks after a game to unwind. Two games weekly, drinks after a difficult practice, and before I knew it, I was inclined to take pleasure in having numerous drinks nightly.

One morning as the first rays of dawn filtered into our bedroom, I woke and she was straddling me and holding an empty whiskey bottle. "This is already gone." It was not a question. I had never before witnessed such intensity on her face.

"Here are the rules, Clint Hurley. You can have two drinks. Your choice, two beers, two drinks of whiskey, two glasses of wine. I don't care which. You want to enjoy two after a game, fine. The other ground rule is that for the foreseeable future you are limited to alcohol three nights a week."

"You know I don't really care for wine," I said. The stern expression on her face informed me that my attempt to diffuse the situation with humor had come up woefully short. I breathed in deeply and said, "Are you saying that I have a problem?"

"No. I'm saying we are not going to allow this," she said, holding the bottle up for emphasis, "to become a problem."

She was quiet for several moments. "Promise me, Clint. I know you would never break a promise to me."

"I promise. I'll go you one better. I'll not have a drink for thirty days."

"I know basketball games take a lot out of you but there are other ways to alleviate the stress."

"Such as?"

She was wearing a pair of my boxers and a tee shirt from church. She rolled to her side and stood by the bed. She removed her clothing and stood perfectly at ease in front of me.

Later, I asked, "What if it's after a road game and it's one o'clock when I come home?"

"You can wake me," she said. "Like you didn't know that anyway."

She hugged me tightly and whispered in my ear. "I just don't want anything to get in the way of our life together."

I didn't either and nothing ever did again until sickness ravaged her body.

I breathed deeply and patted Josie on the head. "Let's go home." She laid down and placed her head in my lap. I put one hand on her head and rubbed her slightly with my fingers and I gripped the wheel with the other.

"O Holy Night" begins to play and I turn the volume up slightly. I recognize the powerful voice of Celine Dion. It was our favorite Christmas Song.

Fall on your knees reaches a crescendo and the tears cascade down my face on to Josie's head. She whimpers slightly but does not stir.

The song ends and I turn the radio off. We are across the bridge now and though I know that I should avoid River Road at night for the concern of colliding with a deer. I turn left anyway. The lights of the Fire Station on the right illuminate the blackness of the night. I say a silent prayer that there will be no need for them to respond to any calls on this special night.

I keep my speed cautiously low. The scattered homes and neighborhoods along the long dark road are sporadically decorated with outdoor Christmas lights. One house has a matching set of tall red and yellow Noel plastic candlesticks on each side of the entrance to their house. They are similar to the ones my father annually placed on the screened in brick porch that served as the main entrance to our home.

Josie barks sharply as she rises up so rapidly that it startles me into tapping the break. She continues to bark and I come to a complete stop to reassure her that all is well. It's then that I notice that approximately thirty feet in front of us there are seven deer crossing the road. I shake my head in slight bewilderment. I sit there with the truck idling, occasionally checking the rear-view mirror but we remain the only vehicle on the road this Christmas Eve, steeped in solitude.

"How did you know girl?"

I swear at this moment I almost expected that dog to speak. She looked intently at me and leaned in with her head, nuzzling my cheek.

The remainder of the trip home proved uneventful. We didn't see another vehicle.

The temperature seems to have dropped rapidly since I walked out of church. We walked inside and I built a nice fire. There was no need to even attempt sleeping in that empty bed. Josie curled up in front of the fire, saturating in its warmth for a few minutes before joining me in the recliner. She most likely would not be bothered by any snapping of the wood that was burning. It was only oak blazing now, though I did use a few split pieces of pine to generate instant coals. The clock on the wall read one o'clock. It was Christmas. "Merry Christmas, Baby," I whispered softly. I fell asleep quicker and deeper than I thought possible on this night.

Four
Clint

"Baby."

Allie was inches from my face. Her face so radiant that it surpasses the most beautiful sunsets I have ever witnessed. "Don't forget the angel," she said, and then she smiled, as she kissed me delicately on the lips.

I wake. Josie has both paws on my chest. She whines softly and licks my face.

"I guess both of us have to pee." I got up and walked to the back door and opened it. She scurried past me. The sky was gray and t was much colder than the forecast which predicted a high near fifty-five for this Christmas Day. The chilling air made me believe that the weather forecaster took the day off.

I walked slowly back inside to use the bathroom and then into the kitchen. It sure takes longer for my body to loosen up these days. I use to lift weights every other morning. Allie and I had a makeshift gym in our garage, equipped with dumbbells, a workout bench, and an elliptical trainer. I sold all of it with the house. It turned out the couple I sold my home to were workout enthusiasts. They made an offer for me to leave all the exercise equipment behind.

I walk the trails in the woods with Josie each day. I do pushups and sit-ups three days a week, now that the building is over. But my most vigorous workout these days is chopping and splitting wood. Talk about a core workout. Of course, it's not like at this stage of life I'm going to have a six pack. It's probably a good thing that I don't. Can you imagine the women coming out of the woodwork if that were true? My neighbor, Lori, might pitch a tent in my yard and refuse to depart.

I removed bacon and eggs from the fridge and began to cook breakfast. Returning to the refrigerator I took out sweet Italian Sausage and ground turkey. It seemed like a Crock-pot kind of day. Christmas Dinner will be sweet potato chili, a dish a friend of ours at Carolina Beach cooked for us one night. It became a staple in our household.

There was a scratch at the back door. I opened it, and Josie rushed in. She walked straight to the kitchen and waited obediently for her breakfast. I walked to the pantry and gathered a bowl of dog food for her.

I obviously was not paying attention because it's only as I place her bowl of food on the floor that I noticed that there were tiny flakes of snow on her back. She begins to eat and I walked to the nearest window to look out. I couldn't believe what I saw. Snow was falling at such a rate that if it kept up this pace there will certainly be accumulation.

We have had one white Christmas in this area as far back as the records date. It was in 1989 and it shut down a city not accustomed to snow. People complain when the rare event of snow occurs and brings our city to a halt but it makes little economic sense to purchase a bunch of equipment for the rare times we receive more than a dusting of snow.

I continued cooking the bacon and the meats for the sweet potato chili. A glance around the house reminds me that there is no Christmas Tree and not one present wrapped. I sent presents to my grandsons. I didn't bother sending anything to my sons or their wives. Any gift a simple man like me might send would not measure up to their lofty standards.

I dined at the small, rectangular, wooden table that I constructed. I did have to buy chairs as my wood working talents didn't grant me the confidence to take on that project. However, I bought the chairs at a yard sale at a church nearby and I refinished them to match the table.

There's a very polite beggar sitting to my left. "I assume you would like a piece of bacon."

I broke a tiny piece off and gave it to her. She ate it slowly, as if she were savoring it. Next, I slid my plate on the floor with the eggs I saved for her. She began to eat, wagging her tail slightly. I returned to the kitchen area and began slicing the sweet potato, onion, and garlic that the recipe required. Minutes later I was done. I looked up at the skylight and saw the snow falling.

The doorbell rang. I didn't move and I gestured to Josie with my palm down. She remained silent. My first guess was that it was Lori, once again caught up in the spirit of the season or the loneliness of not having someone significant in her life. My truck was parked outside so she would know that I'm home. Regardless, I didn't answer the door.

I heard the muffled sound departing the drive, the sound of a truck that makes me think of UPS or FedEx. I walked to the front porch and saw two boxes. One of them was large and the other is more of a medium size. My sons? That would be a shocker. I stared at the packages and it dawned on me as I tried to ascertain their origin that the best course of action would be to take the packages inside and open them. Josie quickly began to sniff the packages and she seems particularly curious about the smaller one.

It's then that I noticed the smaller package is addressed to Josie Hurley. I knew this dog was intelligent but even I didn't think she was capable of reading. She shoved the box with her nose through the open door into the house. I think she might be attempting to tell me something as I stood dumbfounded trying to understand why these packages are here. Ours is probably not the only home in which the dog is obviously the brightest resident.

Josie began barking furiously—her attention bouncing back and forth from the box to me. I retrieved the other box and walked inside. Josie was still barking. I reached into my pocket and pull out my ever-present pocket knife passed on by my dad. I opened it and cut the tape on the box. There are treats inside. Jerky, dog biscuits, and dental chews, each contained in a suitable metal container. I opened the one with jerky in it as Josie watched with anticipation.

She sat obediently and gingerly took the treat from my hand. As I pulled the other containers out of the box and placed them on the counter, I notice a bright red envelope at the bottom of the box addressed to Josie.

"Is it okay if I open this for you?"

She barked once her approval.

I opened the card and wince at the familiar writing. I read it out loud.

Josie,
Are you taking good care of my baby? Oh, how much I hated leaving you two but at least I knew that you would look after him. I know you loved me but there was something you felt for him that could never be matched and I was okay with that. I love you sweet girl.
Merry Christmas,
Mom
PS: Tell Daddy that these treats should last you for several weeks, not a few days.

I sat on the bar stool in front of the counter and tried to take it all in. I looked at the other box and if the dog received a card with presents, I think it's safe to say that I have as well.

I began to cut into the box. Opening the flaps, I saw my card is on top. It's one of those times where you know that you have to do something and in this case that was to read the card. There was another part of me that just did not know if I was prepared to handle the ordeal of a letter from my dead wife.

I take the card and walked to the fireplace, and turn my back to it, soaking in the heat, as I open the card.

Clint,

This is one of those times in life that I have chosen a course of action and yet I'll debate whether it's the right thing to do until I breathe my last, which will not be long. I know you need answers, and I am going to do my best to give them to you.

By the time this reaches you I'll have been in Heaven for approximately one year. I know I am well, free, and happy to be in my eternal home, but at the same time I am just as sure there's a void of not having you with me. You remain the love of my life.

I wonder if you're living in the log cabin on the land we purchased long ago. I hope so. The undertaking of building the cabin I hoped would keep you busy. I didn't want you to sit around and be sad. The thought of that now breaks my heart as I write this last love letter to you.

Assuming that the cabin is finished, I think you need another project. I heard you talk about trains and how they reminded you of the good times in your childhood. I saw where you looked online at this particular train set many times. Well, I think it's time for you to construct this and sit back and watch the trains roll.

Clint, you do the best you can until you join me. There will be a time when we are never separated again.

I love you always,

Allie

PS: No more than two drinks.

I folded the card and placed it back inside the envelope. Josie sat silently by. I shook my head slowly and exhaled deliberately. I managed to chuckle at the last line of the card. She was always in charge. Even now.

I rose and walked back to the box and pulled the first package out. It was an N scale model train set neatly packaged with cars, a locomotive, track, controller and power pack. The locomotive was bright yellow and blue as was the dummy locomotive. There are three less colorful passenger cars.

I placed the box on the counter and begin to pull other smaller packages out. One was a bright blue and yellow caboose. She always did like colorful things. There were landscape accessories and it was clear I would have quite the project to undertake this winter.

Josie walked to the back door and barked. It took me back to the night that she learned to bark when she needed to go out. She learned as a puppy to walk to the back door at our home at Carolina Beach. She would stand and look at that door knob as if she were thinking, if only I had thumbs.

One night, Allie saw her and told her that she was coming, but her phone rang. She took a quick call and forgot about letting Josie out. She went to bed and was watching videos on her phone. Laughing at silly videos. It was disturbing at times as I always read novels before going to sleep and desired the room to be still. Today, I would give all I have to be interrupted by her childlike laughter.

I was loading the dishwasher that night, and when I finished, I walked down the hall to the bedroom. That's when I watched as Josie entered our bedroom and barked three times indignantly at Allie.

"You forgot to let her out?"

Allie's eyes opened wide. "You don't think?"

I nodded my head and let her out, and from that day forward, she learned to bark instructions if her humans didn't move quickly enough to suit her.

Josie waited at the back door. Grabbing my coat and phone, we walked outside and soon we were on the trail through the woods that led to the river. I patted my left thigh and she remained on heel. The snow seems to be picking up in its intensity.

I stopped short of the river near a bench I built last month. "Scout," I say to her and she took her cue of freedom and began to roam.

The trees were turning a radiant white before my eyes. I know our area was heavily populated with northerners who moved here to escape snow, but for those of us who grew up in this area, snow is a special treat.

I gazed across the river. The pristine snow accumulating on the bank of the other side was solid white and next to the brackish water of the river it lent an exquisite contrast.

I looked at the bench which now had two inches of snow covering it. There's a fire pit in front of it and wood is stacked off to the side. I had cleared a small circle around this area last month, with the thought that I would sit here and read a good book with a roaring fire to enjoy.

I watched the snow continue to fall, and it appeared that it would not let up anytime soon. I reflected upon the rare times that it snowed when my sons were little. The simple fun of snowball fights and eating snow cream their mother made. I wondered when or if I'll see them again. Wade was so full of pride and caring about how others perceive him. I don't know exactly what made him that way. He certainly didn't receive that from his parents, and sadly his brother fell in line right behind him.

"Josie, come girl." I didn't even have to raise my voice because even though I can't see or hear her I knew that she was close.

My phone begins to play '*I can only Imagine.*' I retrieved it from my worn saddle color, LL Bean barn coat. It was Bryan.

"Hey, buddy."

"How are you doing?"

"I'm managing." There's silence and I don't want him feeling sorry for me, especially on a day when he's with his family celebrating Christmas. "It's snowing."

"You're kidding."

"No. It's pretty amazing. God, how Allie would have loved this." My voice caught as I struggled to choke back the emotion.

"I know she would. I wish I could help you."

"You do that every day, old friend."

"How can that be possible?" he asked.

"Josie."

"She's a good one. I'm glad she's with you."

"Please end this call and enjoy your family, Bryan. I'm doing okay. I don't want you, or anyone else to feel sorry for me. I had the love of my life for so long. I can't curse God now that he saw fit to take her home. It was my privilege to be with her as long as we were. You know we never spent a night apart. Even when she was in the hospital, I stayed all night." It hit me that Bryan had spent a lot of his career traveling and away from home. I should have not said that.

"Bryan, I'm sorry. I know your job required a lot of traveling. I didn't mean anything toward you in a despairing manner."

"I know that. No apologies needed. Not now. Not ever." He paused and I heard background voices. "They are calling me. I think that it's time to open presents."

"Please tell everyone Merry Christmas." Josie sat beside me—upright and alert. She had settled in so silently that I hadn't even noted her presence

I was in the process of saying bye and ending the call.

"Hey, Clint."

"Yes."

"I love you."

I nodded my head. That's kind of silly isn't it? Bryan can't see that.

"I know buddy. Same here. Bye." I looked at my watch, a worn Seiko that must be thirty years old and the band has been replaced multiple times. I thought about my sons again. The last time they were home they wore Rolex watches that I would wager cost twenty thousand dollars and it kept no better time than my old Seiko. It's more than that. My watch is a gift from their mother. I wonder if they think often of her. She tried to talk to them about where their lives were and how it was more important who you carried in your heart than the trappings of this life. They listened, though they didn't heed her advice any more than they did mine. I quit trying after a while. They were grown men and they would either find their way or not.

They both attended huge mega churches. I questioned if they attend to worship or to just be part of a yet another affluent social setting with a plethora of possible business contacts.

There was an interview on television recently with Dylan's pastor. He wears exquisite suits and I'm pretty sure his watch is an even nicer Rolex than the ones my sons wear.

Recently that same pastor and his wife had a twenty-thousand square-foot mansion constructed on fourteen acres outside of Columbia. Three swimming pools, two guest houses, and of course it's all gated and secured. He rationalized the purchase by talking about all the good he and his wife did. The missions they funded. How their home was paid for with their personal investments. I must give the man credit. He told all of this to the reporter without sweating or stammering. He probably rehearsed that speech a few times. Like many people in this life if you repeat something often enough, you might begin to believe it yourself. I never was good at lying to myself or anyone else for that matter.

Naturally, Dylan thought it was fine for his pastor to enjoy all these possessions, and I don't begrudge anyone nice things. I understand the gated community. Everyone needs their privacy, especially when you become as famous as this man. But no one needs all that for a home. Billy Graham didn't need it and neither does he.

Dylan and his wife became friends with the minister and his wife. Once again, my youngest son is struck with celebrity—much like he has idolized his older brother for all of his life. It saddens me to think that he could have hardly chosen a worse example to follow than his own brother.

Josie and I walked back to the cabin in quietness as the snow continues to fall.

By early afternoon the walls of the cabin were closing in, and I wanted to see the snow again. I dressed in a rain repellant pull over coat with a hood. Josie, thanks to her mom, wore her own rain coat for times we had to take her out in the rain and cold. It's a hideous shade of neon yellow. I guess she wanted to make sure that I didn't lose sight of her.

I carried a flat shovel to clean the snow from the bench, performed that task, and then proceeded to build the nice fire that we enjoyed. I brought the Bible, a devotional book, and the latest novel by Greg Iles. I read, prayed, and soaked up nature. Josie occasionally ventured off but never tarried very long without returning to check on me. Finally, she had enough of exploring and lay on the other end of the bench with her head in my lap enjoying my rubbing her head.

"Josie, this has been a hard year, as I knew it would be, but with the help of God and your company, I've made it this far. I don't know what I would have done without you. You're an angel from God as far as I'm concerned."

The faint light this day had offered was fading. I looked through the trees to the river. The scenery reminded me of a Bob Timberlake painting. I really didn't want to go back inside but I was growing hungry and I wager that my counterpart is as well.

"Sweet girl, are you hungry?"

She lifted her head slowly and looked into my eyes. She would choose to stay on this bench with me and be ravenous than to venture elsewhere for food. I think it safe to say God knew what was coming when Bryan gave this wonderful creature to me.

"Let's go, Josie."

She sat up on the bench and I began to gather my books. The Bible was the last one I picked up and for some reason that I don't know, I opened it. The pages fell open to the Book of Acts and my eyes honed in on Chapter 12, Verse 8. *Then the angel said to him, "Put on your clothes and sandals." And Peter did so. "Wrap your cloak around you and follow me," the angel told him.*

Angels seemed to be somewhat of a theme today that began with a morning dream. I looked toward the river once again. The light continued to diminish and complete darkness would soon encase the wintry landscape. I caught a glimpse of something yellow upstream in the river floating along with the current. The trees were still and it was so quiet that the only noise I could hear was the snow falling and the soft sound of the fire. It was a dreamlike moment. My mind drifted to a place of calm and peace, I have not known since Allie's departure. I waited a few moments savoring the feeling, but darkness was near and we had to go.

***

Turning from the river I take a step toward the cabin with Josie beside me. She gives off a strange noise that I have not heard previously from her. It's like a very curious whimper and I notice raised hackles on her back. There's a white figure in front of me several yards away but how could that be? Everything is blended now into a maze of white but still the outline of a figure seems to remain on the trail. I don't live without protection and right about now I wished I'd brought my revolver. I decide that I might as well face whatever might be in front of me. Taking a step, I hear a voice that seems to be a whisper from the trees above. "Turn around."

I'm trying to comprehend what is occurring and then the figure vanishes. I don't understand any of this. Is my mind playing tricks on me? Josie whimpers and nudges my leg. My heart rate is accelerated and I'm afraid to turn around, fearing something or someone might be behind me. I'm in deep contemplation about what is occurring when Josie barks sharply once, then again. She turned back toward the river and is fixated on something.

I turn around. The snow has relented greatly in just a few scant moments. There are a few flakes still dancing over the river but it appears this unannounced snow storm is winding down. I see the slightest sliver of orange through the clouds. And then I understand.

The orange streak touches the yellow I saw moments ago and in that split second, I realize it's a yellow kayak. It makes no sense. Josie has broken from me without command and is thirty feet in front of me before I head toward the river, pausing briefly to place my books on the bench. I think I hear a faint sound but I'm not sure. I continue moving and Josie is down the bank racing toward the river. My heart is a pounding jackhammer. I negotiate the bank cautiously. She's at the water's edge and barking continuously. The last flicker of sun is enough for me to see that the yellow kayak, moving our way, contains a small figure. The kayak will be past us in just a moment as the steady current is moving it along at a fair pace. The person is so small that it must be a child. I'm unsure of what to do. A child, in a kayak on the river on a snowy Christmas Day? This is like a scene from a movie but there's no Matt Damon to rescue her. There's only an old man and his young dog. As I try to figure out what to do the situation turns brusquely grave. The child leans too far to one side toward us and the kayak capsizes. The tiny figure struggles to stay above water as the kayak floats away from her, carried away with the current.

"Josie, with me," I command as I move quickly along the bank. We will get one shot at this. "Lord, please be with us." Josie follows along. The child's head dips below the water, coming toward us. I point slightly diagonally away from the child, who I now can see is a girl. I pray Josie understands what I'm doing. If she takes off in a direct path toward the child, she will miss her and the current will carry the child past her.

The command for Josie to retrieve is be back. I point in the direction I want her to go. "Be back, Josie. Be back." She leaps into the river and begins to swim furiously. She's thirty feet out and the girl is floating her way. The child's head pops up out of the water and I shout to her to grab the dog's collar.

I'm now in the water up to my knees. The wintry cold I don't feel. You know how you watch a wreck unfold and you twist and turn your body in hopes it can be avoided or maybe more applicable for me when a big shot is taken in a basketball game and you use body language to try to coax the ball into the basket. That's what I do now as I watch. Closer and closer she drifts and it appears as if she will be past Josie by the time she gets there. "Right," I command Josie. I know every instinct tells her to swim straight toward the girl, but she obeys and swims diagonally. They meet and the girl reaches out but she misses the collar and her hand merely brushes Josie's back. She drifts slightly past Josie but somehow Josie has another wind and quickly catches up to the girl.

"Grab her collar," I yell.

The little girl reaches out and snags the collar. I'm up to my waist in the cold river. Josie is slowly making progress toward me, but is laboring. As much as I want this child saved, I sure don't want to lose my dog today. Twenty feet away and Josie keeps paddling. The girl appears to be limp and Josie is literally towing dead weight. "Come on, girl." They are close now, but Josie is in trouble. Then both their heads dip below the river in the same instant. "No. God, no!"

I leap into the murky waters and with one hand I grab the collar and pull Josie up, while grabbing the jacket the girl is wearing with the other. Josie's head is up and she's swimming. "Home," I tell her but even as I say it, I know she'll never leave me in this dark river. I now have both hands on the girl and I float her above the water and work my way toward the shore. Josie follows. Finally, my feet find the shore where I collapse with the little girl.

I look down at the face of this child. She has such smooth looking skin, the color of mocha. Her hair is braided in cornrows. She appears to be about the age of my grandsons. Regardless, even in her present state she's beautiful.

Her eyes open. She looks up at me and says softly—her voice raspy no doubt from the water she has swallowed. "You won't hurt me too will you, mister." I was so exhausted and overcome with emotion. I couldn't find my voice.

We made it to the bank and then into the woods. I had to get her to the cabin quickly to dry her off and have her warmed by the fire and call 911. But moving swiftly is not something a man at my age does, especially when carrying a child. It takes us several minutes to reach the cabin.

Struggling, we make it inside and I reached for my phone, and then it occurred to me that the phone that was in my coat pocket is now in the river. First things first. Strip the wet clothes from her and put her in a warm shower. There's no bathtub here, only shower stalls. I know what must be done but I sure wish there was a woman around to remove her clothes. She's breathing and her eyes are open. How can I convince her that I'm no one to fear?

"I don't know what has happened to you but I promise you I won't hurt you. We have to remove your wet clothes. You've got to warm up. I'll build a fire for you to sit by."

She eyes me warily as her body shivered with cold and probably fear. I wish she was not so fatigued so she could do this on her own but she might collapse in the shower. I wonder how long she was in the river. She appears to be in shock from suffering such an ordeal on a day when she should be spoiled with gifts and surrounded with people she loves. A thought strikes me. We bought a shower seat for Allie when she was so weak that she needed to sit down to bathe. It's in a storage closet right outside the bathroom. I put the toilet seat down and said, "Please sit here." Placing her on the seat I said, "Josie, with her." Josie walks over and sits in front of the girl. The little girl reaches out and touched Josie's snout and says in a barely audible voice, "Thank you, Josie."

I retrieve the seat and set it in place. I turn to the little girl. "What's your name?"

"Jasmin," she says weakly.

I don't know how to do this. I raised sons—not little girls and especially one who likely has reason to fear me. Weariness was consuming me and I knew I had to remove her wet clothes and get dry myself.

"Jasmin, we need to take your clothes off and get you in the shower. You can sit on that seat because I know you're tired."

She nods and I begin to remove the light jacket that she is wearing. Underneath that she has on a gray tee shirt and some worn jeans. She is so weary she is of little help in the process. I pull the wet shirt over her head. I work her jeans off as she stared off into space.

She looks at me and says, "Mister," and then her voice trails away.

"Jasmin, please look at me." She looks wearily into my eyes.

"My name is Clint Hurley. I can't imagine what you have been through. All I can give you is my assurances that I mean no harm. I'll not hurt you or do anything wrong to you."

She studies my eyes searching the truth I know to be there and hope that she can see that as well. She nods softly. "Will you keep the others from hurting me?"

I nod.

"No, say it."

"I'll protect you from whomever it is that frightens you. You have my word."

She nods her head and says softly, "Okay."

I guess she has no other options other than to trust me—an old man and a complete stranger.

"Okay, I'm going to help you onto the shower seat. Don't attempt to stand. You can take your underpants off in the shower. Just throw them on the floor. I'll get everything. The soap and shampoo—whatever you need is right where you can reach them, okay?"

"Where will you be?"

"I'm going to find you some dry clothes. I don't have anything for a little girl but I have two grandsons and I believe there are some pajamas they left that for some odd reason my wife kept."

"Where is she?"

I shake my head and said, "She died last Christmas."

"I'm sorry," she offered.

I turn the shower on and wait for it to be warm but not too hot. She is trembling and so am I. I worry about hypothermia and I'm no nurse but I think it's best to warm the body temperature up gradually. I stare at the wall ahead—so uncomfortable but then I imagine she is as well. She's just too exhausted for it to be a priority. The water is warm, and I close the shower curtain. "You take your time. I'll be outside. There's a big bath towel right outside and I'll give that to you when you're finished. Just call out."

She looks so weary and I worry she might fall off that seat. "Josie." She comes immediately and I realize I forgot to remove her coat. I take it off quickly and tell her to sit and watch the girl. I opened just enough of the shower curtain so she could see. "With her," I command.

I walk to my bedroom and shed all my wet clothes. I put on some sweat pants and a sweat shirt. My shower has to wait. I find the clothes my Allie saved. They were X-Men pajamas and I thought they might even fit. Maybe a little big but at least they are dry.

I began quickly making a fire. Soon the kindling wood and pine cones are burning. I go back to the bathroom. "Are you okay?"

"Yes," she called softly.

"I found some pajamas that I believe will fit you. I'm going to place them on the toilet seat."

"Do I have to come out now? I was really dirty."

"No. Take your time." I place the pajamas on the toilet seat.

I go back to the fire and added some split pine for instant heat that is sorely needed on this frigid Christmas night.

I sit in my recliner; the weariness consumes me and I drift off to sleep.

***

I felt someone patting my shoulder. She wore the pajamas and was no longer shivering.

"You feel better?" I asked.

"I'm hungry," she said.

"Okay. Follow me." She walked behind me to the table and I pulled a chair out for her. She sat down and I retrieved a bottle of water from the fridge and a bowl of chili from the Crock-pot. I placed them both in front of her.

She gulped down the water first and I got her another bottle. Hurriedly she began to eat.

"Jasmin, slow down. I know you're starving and probably dehydrated but I don't want you to get sick. You need this nourishment to stay down so eat slowly. When you finish this bowl, we will wait an hour or so and make sure it all stays down and then you can have more."

"The food won't run out?"

I could not help it. Tears rolled down my cheeks at what kind of ordeal this poor beautiful child must have been through. "No, sweetheart. The food will not run out."

I didn't realize that I was so drained that I was leaning on the table with both hands. As my tears slowed, I felt the hand of the little girl rest delicately on top of mine.

"You need to be dry too. You and Josie both. I'll wait here for you."

"Don't go anywhere," I said foolishly.

"I got no place to go."

I placed some oak logs on the fire and I took Josie to my bedroom and put her in the shower with me. When we were both clean and dry, I walked back to the kitchen and I saw the empty bowl and water bottle. She was not at the table. I was startled. But Josie calmly walked to the fire and the little girl was sound asleep in my recliner. I walked to the closet, retrieved a blanket and covered her up. She didn't stir.

I speculated about what to do. Should I contact authorities but I had no phone and I was not leaving her. And at this moment I didn't trust anyone else with her care.

Josie and I ate our dinner. Later we both lay on the couch. We would sleep here tonight where we could keep watch on the girl from the river.

Five
Clint

The pink light seeped in from the false dawn, waking me for good from an even more fitful night of sleep than was customary. Each time during the night that I woke, I rose and walked the few steps to check on her. Josie accompanied me each time and stared intently at our unforeseen guest. It was as if she were trying to decide what we were meant to do with this little girl. She's not alone in those thoughts.

To my knowledge, Jasmin never made any movement or sign that she even knew I was present. Exhaustion had rendered her to a place of deep slumber and hopefully she was free in her dreams from the trepidation that compelled her to imperil her life to escape her tormenters, whoever they might be.

I touched her forehead and once again I was relieved that her body temperature appeared to be normal. What was I going to do today in regards to this little one who nearly drowned in the shadowy waters of the river?

I walked quietly to the back door and opened it. Josie hurried outside for her morning ritual. I stepped out onto the porch. The sun was close to making its arrival. The light through the trees toward the river was a mixture of deep pink and orange. It was spectacular against the radiance of the snow that cloaked the landscape. I longed to be able to enjoy the splendor on this day after Christmas but my mind was inundated with thoughts of our visitor.

Josie was in the trees and I lost sight of her as my mind mulled over my options for this day. The easy solution was for me to simply call the authorities. If I took the easy course of action and it resulted in her being returned to a dire situation, I would never forgive myself.

I was so lost in contemplation that I heard nothing, save the slight wind rustling through the trees. I felt a little hand tug on mine. "I'm hungry. Could I have some more of what you fed me last night?"

I looked down and those dark soulful eyes gazed at me with hope that I might meet the simplest of her needs. "I am honored that you liked my sweet potato chili so much but how about if I cook breakfast for you? Eggs, bacon, hash browns, and maybe some biscuits. Now, I can't cook biscuits from scratch like my Allie could but I can twist, pop, and bake those that come in the Hungry Jack cylinder."

"I can have all that for breakfast?"

I nodded. Josie popped up on the porch and put her snout on the little girl's tummy. Jasmin rubbed her with her free hand.

My mind drifted toward my morning routine of devotion time. I realized my Bible and other books were still on the bench. It didn't appear to have snowed anymore after I brought Jasmin inside so maybe they would not be damaged.

"I left my books on the bench last night. I'm going to retrieve them and I'll be right back, okay?"

She shook her head slightly and grasped my hand harder.

"You don't have a coat and it's cold. You need to be inside." She refused to let go of my hand.

I reclaimed my hand and we walked inside and I grabbed the throw blanket from the couch. I wrapped it snugly around her and held both arms out. She nestled into them. I picked her up. She was skinny but not terribly underweight. She wrapped her arms around my neck. I walked the trail to the bench—Josie healing by my side. We stopped and observed a cardinal perched on an oak tree limb in front of us. His red coat gleamed radiantly, highlighted by the brilliant snow.

We watched silently for a few moments until he flew away. We continued on toward the bench and once there I gathered my books. They seemed no worse for the wear. My bible was a Christmas present from many years past, from Allie, and I was relieved that it was not ruined. I so wish she was here. This is the type of situation she would take charge of and I would follow orders. As much as we loved each other all through our years together we trusted each other equally as much. I don't mean trust in relation to other women or men but we trusted our hearts—the very depths of it to each other. Even in our disagreements there was never a desire to injure. Now, I am not one of those old people who tell you we never had a cross word in our marriage and quite frankly I never believed any of those folks that offered such absurd claims.

The sun was emerging now and the color display was departing rapidly. The bright light reflecting off the snow hurt my eyes. I held her with one arm and the books with my other.

Approaching the back deck there were two blue jays feeding from a bird feeder that I brought with me from Carolina Beach. I made a mental note to refill it later. Our native birds are not use to foraging for food in these conditions. I would provide them a little assistance.

The wind swirled around and I doubted the temperature to be more than twenty degrees. The brisk winds quickly produced rich blue skies.

We walked inside and I placed her back in the recliner. She had begun to shiver slightly on the walk back and I covered her once again with the blanket. I stoked the fire and added some logs. Aided by the hot coals from an all-night fire it didn't take long for the blaze of the fire to return.

I turned the television on and gave her the remote. "I'll start cooking."

She didn't respond and like many children she was soon immersed watching the television. I glanced at the screen and saw that it was on the Hallmark channel. The movie playing was *'Christmas with Tucker'* and James Brolin was having a heart to heart talk with his grandson. Allie and I had watched this particular movie probably a half dozen times. It was one of our favorites.

"That's who you look like," she said, pointing to the screen.

"Do you mean James Brolin?"

She eyed me with a look of perplexity.

"Do you mean the old guy in the coat with the gray hair and wrinkles?"

"Yes, you look like him," she answered emphatically.

"Thank you. But even when I was much younger, I doubt I was ever as good looking as James Brolin is in his seventies."

"I bet your wife didn't think so," she replied quickly.

She had me there. I walked to the kitchen and began retrieving the needed items from the fridge. I turned the Keurig coffee maker on and started the other items. As I monitored the progress, I pulled a stool to the counter and began to read from the book of James. There were a few scriptures that seem to speak to my current predicament.

> *What good is it, my brothers, if a man claims to have faith but has no deeds? Can such faith save him? Suppose a brother or sister is without clothes and daily food. If one of you says to him, "Go, I wish you well; keep warm and well fed," but does nothing about his physical needs, what good is it? In the same way, faith by itself, if it's not accompanied by action, is dead.*

My mind ran through scenarios as I turned the bacon. A young girl is so desperate to escape her circumstances that she steals a kayak and takes off in the river, and not only on the coldest of days, but on a special day when kids should be warm, safe, and happy. Who had frightened this child so much that she would take such risk?

One thing for certain, someone is looking for her. A child does not go missing on Christmas Day without it being big news. I wonder where the kayak came to rest. Hopefully the current took it far from here.

I assumed that it was no accident that this child was currently out of danger. God had delivered her to a place out of harm's way, placing me in a vicarious predicament. I thought of something Allie occasionally said. He will not bring you to something without walking you through it. You just have to trust.

Later we ate breakfast and Jasmin ate heartily but she remembered me telling her last night to eat and drink slowly. It's apparent that this is a really intelligent child. I don't know what I base that on other than just watching her observe things and the look of an older soul, housed in her small frame.

She obviously needed clothes and all the other items little girls require but I could scarcely take her shopping. Maybe the first thing to do was to find out where she came from.

She finished eating and took her plate into the kitchen and washed it off before placing it in the dishwasher. I sipped on the coffee in my brown mug that had worn cursive letters stating the verse of Jeremiah 29:11. *For I know the plans I have for you," declares the Lord, "plans to prosper you and not to harm you, plans to give you hope and a future.* The other side of the mug had a small white cross.

And as we often do, we conveniently hone in on a verse that makes us feel good. I am no different but one day I noticed that two scriptures later in verse 13 there was an equally important scripture that tied in well with these plans he has for us. *You'll seek me and find me when you seek me with all your heart.* I make no claims to being a teacher of the bible but even a man like me realizes that the word "all" sure does appear quite frequently.

"God, what I am supposed to do? Someone is looking for her. The law is certainly involved and I would just as soon not spend my last days on this earth in jail."

It was only then that I realized that these were not thoughts that I was debating but rather I had voiced them out loud. I sensed her eyes on me. I really don't want to turn her way right now.

"Do you believe in God?"

I turned my head curiously toward her.

"I believe in God and that's why I got in that boat yesterday. I don't even know how to paddle. I've seen it done before by people on the river. I noticed the current was moving along pretty fast so I just assumed the water would take me away from where I was and it did. That was good because I couldn't work the paddle very well."

This little one amazed me with how she spoke so articulately. I walked over to the couch and sat down across from her. She changed the channel to the local station and I saw a reporter with the Cape Fear River behind her. The camera panned to the yellow kayak that was on the shore line not far from here.

The next frame moved to another reporter in a different location. The reporter appeared to be no older than a teenager. He was with a man I recognized. Charlie Rind is the United States representative for our region and he has lived in Wilmington his entire life, except for the years he spent obtaining his education at Campbell University, which is less than two hours away. He's like many politicians. He practiced law for a few years, ran for office and now he's serving his twelfth term. Yet another career politician—just what our country needs.

The report was live and they were fumbling to be ready for an interview. His face was pale white and he appeared forty pounds overweight. He had a bulbous nose with noticeable blue veins and wavy hair as white as the snow outside. The wind kept blowing it and he kept pushing it away from his eyes.

He seemed to be okay for a politician and he cares a lot about our local environment. He fought any oil drilling off our coast with such a passion that I believe he was sincere about it.

Charlie Rind is quite the family man. His wife, Althea and he could never have children, so they adopted several kids.

The camera panned around, showing a gray mansion with huge white pillars surrounded by a black wrought iron fence. There were several majestic live oak trees, bordering three sides of the home. Well-manicured plant beds filled the space between the live oaks. Politics pays quite well, I surmised when all the perks are factored in.

"That's the place I escaped from."

Did I just hear that? This situation just keeps getting better by the moment. I not only have a child under my roof that probably is assumed dead but to top it off I have a powerful United States Representative's child. Regardless of what Jeremiah 29:11 states, I won't even try to convince you right now that I had confidence in my future. I knew if I said that very thing out loud and Allie was here, she would say, "Your future. What about that child's future?" As she most often was, she would be correct.

The sound of a helicopter grew louder and I knew it was not part of the television. It came from the river. I walked out back and looked over the trees. The helicopter was flying back and forth along the river. I walked back inside.

Jasmin sat on the couch. Josie had moved with her and sat on the floor in front of her. I sat down beside her. I could hear the voice of Charlie Rind but it was not the smooth, velvet intonation I was accustomed too. He was sincerely broken as he begged anyone that might have seen Jasmin to please call 911. They showed a photo of Jasmin.

"He hurt you?"

"No," she replied, as she shook her head. "She did." She pointed to the screen. I felt her draw close to me and I placed my arm around her. Her entire body was locked in a tense state.

The congressman's wife was beside him now. He held her with his arm and she collapsed into him. "Please help us. I can't believe that she has drowned. Please," she added, as she wept bitterly.

I turned the television off and thought about the course this conversation needed to take. I scratched my head and searched for words. Jasmin rose from the couch and stood in front of me and then she turned around. She lifted the back of the pajama top and I saw the marks on her back. Long thin streaks of injury. Bruises that had faded from the time of assault. She turned around to face me with a very matter of fact expression. "She likes to hit me there and on my butt. She also has a ruler that she will pop my head with at times."

I never saw those marks last night because I was so busy averting my eyes from a child's mostly naked body. I shook my head. "Does the man hit you?" I hesitated before asking another question that I really was not certain I desired an answer too. "Does the man hurt you in other ways?"

"You mean my private area?"

A small child had just embarrassed the heck out of this old man. I shook my head softly, breathed deeply and said, "Yes, I mean your private areas."

"No."

I exhaled in relief.

"She always makes sure the injury is covered."

"You never showed anyone?"

"Once I showed the maid. I thought maybe since Mother Rind treated her so poorly and since she was black like me, that she might help. She told Mother Rind and I received my worst beating ever. Mother Rind promised me that if I ever told anyone, especially

Mr. Rind, that she would take care of me in a way I would never forget."

I shook my head again. Never have I been able to comprehend the evil that leads one to inflict pain on children.

"What happened to your family?"

"I don't have any. I never knew my dad and Mom died of cancer two years ago. I have no brothers or sisters. I was placed in a children's home and the Rinds visited one day and they were looking for another child. Everyone wanted to be chosen, including me. Mom use to say to be careful what you wish for. I didn't understand what she meant at the time but I do now."

"How long have you been with them?"

"Since July."

"Does she beat all the children?"

She shook her head. "Not like she beats me."

"Mr. Rind?"

"He's in Washington a lot and when he's home, she acts different. She's nice to us—hugging and kissing us and telling us how much she loves us. That's almost worse than the beatings," she said, her voice trailing off, before adding, "She makes us clean and work all the time. If we don't do our chores correctly, we don't eat dinner that night."

"How many children are living there?"

"Three. There are others who grew up and have moved away. The Rinds paid for their college and they still send them money at Christmas each year. I had to put all the checks in the envelope and address them last week. It was five thousand dollars each." She stopped for a moment before adding, "There are pictures of all the children that lived there in the great room. My picture made the thirteenth one on the wall."

I deliberated for a few moments. She was back beside me now. "Do any of those children ever visit? The older ones that have moved on."

"No, and I heard Mr. Rind say once that he didn't understand it. They did sometimes visit him in Washington but they never returned to that home."

I nodded my head and understood. They had bad experiences as well but maybe not to the degree that Jasmin has endured. They might have even cared for Mr. Rind but not his wife. They probably enjoyed the perks and let's face it five grand every Christmas can buy a lot of silence for most people. I recalled a news show I watched once that featured the Rinds and all their good works. They adopted children with little hope for a bright future. I thought they were doing it out of kindness and maybe Mr. Rind was, but how could he not know about what his wife was doing? Was he really away that much, and was she really that good a performer?

"You don't have to keep me, Mr. Hurley."

"Clint."

"You don't have to keep me, Clint."

"Look at me please."

She turned and studied my eyes. I was this child's hope. Somehow my fears dissipated for the moment. Besides, if I turned away from her, I would live with that selfish decision for the rest of my life. I was already living in the sorrow that Allie was gone. I don't think I am up to adding more troubles to my already crowded mind.

"I don't know how this will work out. But I'm going to do my best to help you."

She reached over and with her small hand and touched my weathered face. "You promise?"

"I promise."

"Is there anyone else that can help us?"

I hated to involve anyone else in this dilemma. Technically, while my heart was in the right place, I'm breaking the law. Involving anyone else meant they would be breaking the law too.

"I'm not sure but for now why don't we both pray for help?"

"Mom prayed all the time. She anointed my head with this oil all the time and prayed for me."

"I'm glad you have good memories of your mom. They will never leave you even when you're old like me. My mom has been gone for a long time and I think of her each day, especially in the early morning when I read my bible and begin each day in prayer. That's what she always did."

I rose and walked to the kitchen to make my second cup of coffee. There was the sound of feet behind me. I recognized Josie's paws clicking on the wood floors but there were two more feet trailing behind me. I pushed the power button on the coffee maker.

"Can I make it for you?"

I turned around and looked down at her. "For as long as you stay here, you're no one's servant, okay?"

"Okay, but you have cooked and helped me and Mom said to always return kindness with kindness."

I chuckled softly. "Okay, let me show you how."

"You don't really think that Mother Rind made her own coffee, do you? You sit down at the table and just tell me what you want in it."

She retrieved the brown coffee mug off the counter, pausing to study the words. She turned to me and it was the first time I witnessed her grin. It was a remarkable sight and I felt myself laughing slightly. "What is it?"

"This is what Mom did when she put the oil right here," she said, pointing to her forehead. "She did a mark of..."

"The cross," I answered.

"Yes. How did you know?"

"I had a Mom also."

She placed the mug in the proper place, loaded the K cup of Caribou Coffee and pressed the button.

She waited and when it was finished, she brought it to me and placed it on the table. "What do you take?"

"Half and half and three packs of stevia that are in that glass container with the metal top."

"This container looks old," she said as she pulled the packets out.

"It's old. It was in the house that I grew up in."

"You kept it because it reminds you of your mom."

I nodded in agreement.

She brought the packets over and tore them open carefully and poured them in my mug. Next, she walked to the fridge and retrieved the half and half out of the door. She picked up the spoon I used earlier that was by the coffee maker, opened the half and half and said, "Tell me when."

She finished by stirring my coffee. She sat there quietly as I drank my coffee and read some more from the book of James. When I finished, she asked, "Now could I please have some more of that chili? I never had anything like it before?"

I smiled and nodded.

"I was what Mother Rind said was a defiant child. You know what that means?"

"Yes."

She continued as if I had not answered. "It means I missed a lot of dinners."

Part Two
Six
Teke

It was late afternoon as I studied my husband, Bret, as he sipped coffee and watched the sunset over the Cape Fear River from our A-Frame home, located in Castle Hayne, North Carolina. Our yellow lab, Jake, lay on the wood floor beside him. We had lived in this house that Bret, with the help of my father, brother and me completed in the late summer of 1967.

Often I sat in the rocking chair beside him and at times like now, I observed him through the kitchen window as I prepared dinner. He never tired of watching the sun bed down on the river. Not as the teen age boy I fell in love with long ago and not now as the distinguished older man he had grown to be.

Many evenings he grilled on the back porch but this afternoon he asked if I would please cook tonight. He was nothing like this when I first met him. He was conceited, arrogant, and his manners were sadly lacking. But I fell desperately in love with him and we watched one miracle after another transform our lives.

He was not a man to waste words but he had been particularly quiet today. Something was weighing on his mind. During the first years of marriage I would have nagged him until he told me what was going on but now, I was okay just waiting. It's not like we kept secrets from each other.

I laughed softly as I thought again of his request to please cook—as if I would not do anything for him. We certainly had been an unlikely pair at one time. It is hard to believe that we are now approaching our sixties. Some people have confessed that they envy what we share with one another. Of course, there are still some narrow-minded critics but at least it was not as dangerous as it once was. With the help of God we overcame all our enemies. I read Isaiah 54:17 often and we lived the verse despite all the obstacles hurled at us. *No weapon forged against you'll prevail, and you'll refute every tongue that accuses you. This is the heritage of the servants of the Lord, and this is their vindication from me," declares the Lord.*

I observed him rub the right side of his hair just above his ear. It was always this side and done at the same pace when he had something on his mind he was trying to sort through. He rose from the chair and walked to the porch edge and placed his hands on the railing. It was as if he wanted a better vantage point to observe that last diminutive bit of light from the sun that was now nestled behind the trees on the other side of the water. He turned around to walk inside, pausing to look at me through the window. He was ready to talk. I had learned to be silent and listen. Something a young girl had not been so adept at long ago.

He opened the door and Jake entered ahead of him and trotted to the living room and lay down on his bed. I checked the lasagna in the oven. Ten more minutes. I turned to him-he is the best-looking man I had ever seen when we first met and he still is today. His hair is still dark but there was almost as much gray peppered into it now. He is tall and heavier then when we first met but it is weight gained through years of work and lifting weights. The men he employed over the years as a contractor respected how he was willing to still perform the actual work. Truth was he would rather have a hammer or a saw in his hand than be cooped up in an office doing paper work.

There was something about his face, the way it was chiseled that imparted strength. And if I lingered on those deep blue eyes of his dinner must just be delayed. He is the only man I had ever known and I would have it no other way. The same could not be said for his history in that area but that was a long ago past and that is where it remains.

"What are you smiling about?"

I didn't realize that I was until he pointed it out. "My handsome husband," I answered.

"Still?"

"More so," I replied with a smile.

He nodded gently his appreciation. He turned back to the river as if he could view it through the blackness that had set in for the night. "The pier has some boards in need of replacing and probably all the railing. Think you might want to help me?"

He already knew I loved doing anything with him. He is for the most part retired as a contractor these days, though he never really said it. He just began turning down jobs and spending more time at home. He is a master craftsman and much of his work these days is spent here or if the church called and mentioned one of the elderly people needed some repair work done, he was happy to perform the work without charging, as long as no one made a fuss about it. He shared a friendship once with an elderly man, Louie, for whom he had tremendous respect and even greater love. I knew Louie was a big part of the reason he had such a soft place in his heart for those older and lacking financial means to maintain their homes.

He didn't come inside to talk about the pier, though I had noticed the boards as well. What can I say? I had picked up a little knowledge in my years of living with a carpenter. I had no trouble with pounding nails for hours beside him and I am quite proficient with a hammer.

I also no longer worked and had not for several years. I was a public-school teacher in the New Hanover County school system for over twenty years. One day he asked me to retire. He knew I loved teaching and he meant it when he asked and not demanded.

He had done quite well building homes and he invested wisely. He particularly had a knack for buying the right individual stocks. I smiled, recalling the line from the movie *Forrest Gump* that alluded to a fruit company. My husband bought five hundred shares of that fruit company back in 1985 when it was two dollars per share. We still owned all that stock plus all the shares gained from the four ensuing stock splits.

I studied and prayed on the matter of retirement for several months. My first reaction, though silent, was no. But when the next August rolled around, I informed the Board of Education that I would not be returning. He was immersed in the construction of a mammoth house on the Intracoastal Waterway in nearby Hampstead for a demanding client.

School began on Tuesday that year and the following Friday he came home from work early. "School buses are all over the place." He looked at me for an explanation as not a word had been shared since his request from several months back.

"I'll honor your request."

"I don't want you to be unhappy with your decision."

"I won't be."

"Thank you."

I never regretted my choice and just as he occasionally helped the elderly with their homes, I helped young children sent my way with their education. I also refused payment. God had paid us enough.

There was one child that lived close by and her mom insisted on bringing over homemade pecan pies when she discovered that was our favorite. I eventually had to inform the lady that she had to stop because my jeans were getting a little too snug. The lady reluctantly agreed but she brought over two for Christmas that year and continued to do so each year after. Her child was now in grad school at Wake Forest.

"Was it too quiet this Christmas, Grandma?" he asked, with a slight smirk on his face, before adding, "Being stuck here with just me."

"Stop calling me Grandma. It makes me feel old."

He smiled and reached out with his strong arms and pulled me in close. I buried my head in his chest and I felt safe and loved as I did each time, he performed this simple gesture.

We were wary of having children, for what they might go through, deriving from parents of different races. These days you saw that frequently but back in the seventies it was not that way. We were in our early thirties when our only child, Victoria was born, named after his grandmother. Vicky lived long enough to see her namesake come into this world. She died three months later.

During the last week of her life, Bret confided his fears to his grandmother about what type father he might be. She touched his face with her pale, spotted, wrinkled hand and said, "Son, you'll do it well. You have already been a father to your little brother and Alex turned out pretty well, don't you think?" She smiled and offered words he would savor forever. "I am so proud of you."

Victoria, who we called Vic, lived in Austin, Texas with her husband, Val and their two children.

"I guess you want me to get to it," he said, releasing me.

"That would be nice," I answered.

"You're so beautiful," he said wistfully.

"Say that again and we are going upstairs right now and you'll be having a late dinner."

"It would not be the first time," he said, with a mischievous smirk that got me every time.

"Remember the guy in Rocky Point that lost his wife last Christmas?" he asked.

"Yes. Clint Hurley."

He shook his head and said, "I had the strangest dream last night. I could see him clear as day. He appeared confused."

"Why don't you drive over in the morning?"

"Will you come with me?"

I waited for an explanation.

"I saw the two of us walking to his log cabin. I could not see him at this point but you know how in a dream sometimes you know someone is there even though you can't see them?" He paused before adding, "It could be nothing. Maybe it's just a silly dream."

I smiled and said, "There's only one way to find out. Now, how about dinner?"

He kissed me softly. "How about upstairs first?"

I looked at him and saw that ever so slight grin. I turned back to the stove and cut everything off and cracked the oven door a bit to let some of the heat out. The food could wait.

I followed him, my hand entwined with his as we walked up the same stairs that we once raced up to be together many years ago.

We lay in bed afterwards. The darkness of the room, illuminated only by the candles I always loved to burn at special times. And every moment of intimacy with my husband was unique. We had done well in taking little for granted. Maybe even more so now that we had lost precious loved ones. I felt his hand wipe the tears from my face that I didn't even realize were present.

"Our first Christmas with just the two of us," he said in a voice, barely above a whisper.

I didn't respond and he continued. "Too much to ask of Vic to pack up her kids and come home. Besides, Austin is Val's home."

I snuggled closer to him and said, "It was good they came at Thanksgiving. And she will visit in the summer."

"But maybe that is not the main reason that we feel this sadness. It's the first Christmas that we have not had a pig picking. Remember that first one? You can't make that stuff up. I guess today it would be a Hallmark movie but not back then."

I heard the wind rustle through the trees, the only interruption in the still night. I was seventeen when I initially came here as a temporary hideaway from those that would do me harm. I lived in Philadelphia back then with my mother Jacky. I loathed the quiet of these woods then, but now I found such tranquility in them. There were no paved roads close by and certainly no neighbors after Bret's grandmother passed away. I thought of the odds of a young city black girl and an old, somewhat cantankerous white woman becoming so close that I felt Vicky was every bit as much my grandmother as she was to Bret and his brother, Alex.

This was all Vicky's property at one time. She gave it all to Bret in her will, drawn up long ago. It was near the end of her life when Bret asked her if she wanted to change the will and divide the property with Alex.

She huffed indignantly, as she was apt to do. "Why give the lawyers money? I come from a time when your word was worth more than contracts, wills or any legal document. You're cut from the same cloth. It was my privilege to watch you raise Alex. I know you're going to say you had help and you did. But truth be known, you never needed any of us for that. You love Vic but not one ounce more than you love your little brother. If he needed a kidney you would give him one of yours and never think twice. When his leg was shattered you would have taken on his pain. People need lawyers to force people to do what is right by signing their name to a piece of paper. You do what is right because that's the man you are. And in return, though you're both adults now, you have a little brother that always has looked up to you with great admiration and he always will. And Alex knows that this place has always meant more to you than to him. Years ago, as a little kid he followed you without question from the luxurious life your father provided to live in the woods out here."

She breathed in deeply and then continued. "Alex would never want to live here. Your child certainly would not. It's yours and Teke's to do with as you please. The way things are spilling out of Wilmington, I'm certain this property would be something the developers would love to get their hands on. And that's fine because I'll be in my forever home. One day we all will be."

92

In the stillness of the night my husband interrupted my thoughts. "I sure do miss your dad. He was as fine a man as I have ever known. Occasionally, when we worked on a job together, he loved to repeat the story of the arrogant white boy that showed up one day and asked for his beautiful black daughter and how close he came to stomping him senseless. He repeated that story one last time this year before he passed away. It was just the two of us. But he was very serious this time and I suspect he knew he would not share this narrative again. He placed that huge strong hand of his on the side of my face and said, 'Son, I never thanked you for coming to my home that day and fighting for my daughter. Thank you. You have been a truly great blessing in my life.'"

I knew, though there were no sounds produced that this was one of the handful of times I'd ever known my husband to cry. I reached over and wiped his tears and said, "He looked at you as his. Money was the bigshot basketball player that the nation knew about, but he was I believe, just as proud of who you were." I smiled and then added, "He sure took some ribbing from the fellows in town about his white son-in-law. Until one day."

"What day?"

"I thought you knew."

"I don't know what you are talking about," he responded.

"You remember his distant cousin, Reggie? The big guy who played football at Georgia."

"Yes."

"Dad went to that market that was on Dawson Street one afternoon. It was when I was still in college. Some of the fellas were hanging out in that area beside the store that had the picnic tables. Dad was close to entering the store and they called for him to come over. Reluctantly, Dad walked over to the group of men. Reggie evidently had enjoyed a few quarts of beer this particular day.

"Reggie started razzing Dad about his white son-in-law and the guys started laughing. As you know, it took a lot to make Dad mad and he tried to excuse himself after a few minutes. He turned to walk away and Reggie put his hand on his shoulder to turn him back around, saying something crude about you in the process.

"Dad turned and hit him so hard in the face that he knocked him over the picnic table. This was a guy that played defensive end in college and had a brief stint with the Buffalo Bills. Everything got deathly quiet. Dad looked at the rest of them. "Anyone else want to say another word about my white son-in-law? There were no takers."

"You were there?" Bret asked.

I shook my head. "I think it was right after Money graduated and he was home from State. Dad swore Money to secrecy and Money never told me until the day after Dad died."

"Did anyone say anything again?"

"What do you think? Of course, Reggie's pride was wounded and he denied that it ever happened or sometimes, his version was that he got sucker punched. He would get drunk and talk about how he was going to even the score but the truth is that he cut a wide berth around my father after that."

Bret cut the lamp on by the bed. "Let's eat dinner. I sure wish it was leftovers from a pig picking but you make really good lasagna."

We rose and slipped our clothes back on. "I know what you mean but perhaps we can focus more on being thankful for all of those many pig pickings that Dad did prepare for all of us. Some poor folks just had turkey," I added.

He nodded at me and smiled. "I sure did love him."

"And he you," I whispered.

Seven
Clint

It's two days after Christmas and I need to somehow find a safe way to purchase the things that this little girl needs. I did wash and dry the clothes that she escaped in but she obviously needed more than that. I didn't hear the helicopters this morning and I speculated as to whether they had called off the search. Maybe the authorities accepted that she probably drowned and her body had been carried away with the swift current and that the waters had not yet chosen to surrender its casualty.

I ordered a new phone yesterday to replace the one I lost in the river. I paid for express shipping and it should be here today. I debated about purchasing clothing for Jasmin online but decided it was too risky. The order would be on my credit card and of course the delivery date. The authorities might assume Jasmin had drowned but they certainly would not rule out the chance that someone had abducted her.

I was not certain of anything at this point. I could venture out to shop and pay cash. As if I know anything about the things a little girl requires. I heard a door close in the drive. Jasmin looked at me warily from the couch. She walked to the bedroom that she slept in last night and closed the door.

I walked to the door and looked through the glass portion. It was Bret and Teke Marin. They were known throughout most the region, married since they fell in love as teenagers in 1967. Nothing newsworthy about two young people falling in love but there was in this case, particularly during a time in the South where integration was slow to come and men hid cowardice behind white robes and tormented those of color and those that befriended them.

95

Bret Marin's father was once one of the most powerful men in the state and the last thing he wanted to see was one of his sons marrying a black girl, regardless of how beautiful and talented she was.

They had overcome opposition from both white and black communities to be together and along the way they had not only survived but thrived.

I don't know Bret well but I felt a sense of calm as they approached. I met him when he showed up one day and wanted to help with the cabin out of professional curiosity. Teke came with him the next time he arrived. She has a lean body that belongs on a much younger woman. I also could see what they shared for one another as I recognized it well. A love that's powerful, secure, and as natural as the sun bedding down for its nightly slumber over the river.

I opened the door and welcomed them inside. Better to just act natural and see what they had on their minds. I offered them coffee, which they accepted and minutes later they sat on the couch while I sat in the love seat across from them. We chatted easily about the cabin, the extreme weather, and the holidays.

I could tell that Bret had something on his mind and that he was debating with how to broach the subject of why they were here. A few minutes more of meaningless conversation was all that his wife could take, and what she said next, flabbergasted me

"You have the little girl that most people think drowned in the river on Christmas Day."

We sat frozen and no one seemed to know what to say. Teke watched and waited and when it was apparent that it might be a while before either of the men in the room found our voice, she forged ahead. "Clint, there are two plates on the table. One coffee cup and one glass. Two sets of eating utensils. Now, I know Josie is smart, but I don't see her sitting at the dining table comfortably handling a fork and a knife."

Teke stood and walked toward the bedrooms. She stopped at the first bedroom and opened the door. The little girl sat on the bed, clothed in an expression of despondency.

"Come with me, Jasmin. We are here to help."

The little girl followed her to where we were sitting. Jasmin sat next to me and I told the story about how this child entered into my life. Bret shared about his dream.

"If you get involved that could lead to trouble and I don't want that."

Teke started to speak but her husband placed his hand firmly on her leg. "We were involved from the moment of the dream and we trust God to watch over all of us."

I studied him and I could sense the strong conviction in his words and in his expression. Teke merely nodded and reached out to hold Bret's hand. Sadness washed over me as I thought of how much I missed holding hands with my wife. We often went to sleep at night with our hands as entwined as our hearts were.

I rubbed my head and said deliberately, "I guess I have no choice. It's not as if Jasmin can stay inside the rest of her life."

"Let's give this some time to play out and formulate a plan," Bret suggested.

Teke said, "I have an idea of how to begin. I can take her to buy clothes and we can change her hairstyle. That might help us buy some time. I have a friend who has a shop between here and Burgaw. We can buy her clothes there. She'll tell no one."

At the mention of this Jasmin moved closer to me. I smiled and then I grabbed her hand and looked in her eyes. "Jasmin, we have to trust someone at some point. I know these people and you can trust them."

Teke spoke to me but her eyes were on Jasmin. "Why don't you bring her to our place sometime today? We'll be home. Bring Josie. She can play with Jake. We have no neighbors and our place is secluded. I'll call my friend and ask her to meet us after store hours.

She closes at five thirty each day. It will be dark by then and we can purchase clothes for her. No one will see her." She paused before adding, "We use to have to hide out long ago. I have not forgotten how."

I nodded my head in agreement.

They walked to the truck as Jasmin and I stood on the porch, watching the truck disappear down the road.

***

It was a little after five that afternoon. "Are you ready?"

Jasmin walked over to me and took my hand. "Tell me again why we should trust them?"

I chuckled slightly. "Just a feeling. That and lots of prayer."

"Anything else?"

"Maybe one day they will share their story. I only know parts of it, though I think that it's safe to say that Teke will do most of the storytelling."

"Do you mean like your wife did?"

"Yes, like my wife did."

"What do you know about their story?"

"I know that when they were young people of different races didn't exactly hang out together and for certain they didn't date or marry."

She studied on my response for a few moments. "My mom dated a white man for a while. I didn't mind."

"Jasmin, I am a simple man with simple beliefs. I believe in God and he doesn't care what color his children are. He looks on our hearts. That is what defines us and makes us who we truly are. People often try to camouflage who they really are. They hide behind deceit, possessions, fashion, makeup—you name it, but God sees our heart. We can never fool him."

"Why do people hide who they really are?" she asked.

"They are fearful they won't be loved."

She was silent as I glanced at the clock. It was nearly five thirty. The sun set twenty minutes ago and the light is fading quickly. I gave her a ball cap. "Put this on."

"For a disguise?"

"Yes."

"That makes sense." She took the hat from me and tried it on. Removing it, she adjusted the back strap to make it smaller, and put it on once again. Satisfied with the fit, she said, "Okay, let's go," in a businesslike manner.

I placed my hand on her head and smiled. "How old did you say you were?"

"Ten."

Shaking my head, I said, "You seem so much older. I guess you have had to grow up fast."

Josie walked beside us as we made our way to my truck. The engine started quickly and I drove away. The sound of the motor is always a pleasant, reassuring hum to me. I could thank my mechanic Bubba for that. He's near my age but still works in the shop behind his home. I think when his time comes; they will find him with his head under the hood of some vehicle with wrench in hand.

I am lulled to quietness as I frequently am when I drive and I fail to see that Lori is standing in her driveway until we are almost to her. "Duck Jasmin!"

She fails to understand quickly enough and I reach over and pull her shoulder toward me. We are past her now and as I look in my rearview mirror, Lori is motioning for me to stop. "Stay down."

I wave at her and keep on driving. "I'm sorry. I should have told you that you might need to keep out of view. That was not very smart on my part."

"Who was that?"

"My neighbor."

"Did she see me?"

"I hope not."

"Would she tell?"

I breathe out deliberately. "I don't know."

She nodded and seems to be in deep thought for several moments. "But we can trust Bret and Teke?"

"Yes."

We drove the rest of the way in silence to Castle Hayne. She remained slouched down in the seat with her head nestled close to Josie.

I drove down the long dirt road passing a well taken care of older home. I had never been to their home before but I recalled Bret telling me that they lived on the river. The long driveway came to an end and my headlights shone on an A-Frame. As we got out of the truck, I could smell the river.

Josie ran off toward some trees, not wanting to miss out on any opportunity to take in fresh aromas. I heard a voice from above. "Keep her on heal."

I looked up and Bret Marin was standing on a small balcony. "I've seen a few coyotes around lately. Best to be safe. Follow the lighted pathway to the front."

I called Josie to my side and we walked together to the front of their home and proceeded up the steps. I stood on the deck and admired the outside of the home. I was not sure I had seen a home in the area that looked anything like this one.

"Come inside," Teke said, as she opened the door.

"Thank you for this," I said.

She shook her head. "We would have never made it without help long ago. It's the least we can do."

She looked down at Jasmin. "Are you ready? I don't want to keep my friend waiting." Her eyes returned to me. "Walk up the stairs and the door that's open is our bedroom. Bret is waiting for you on the balcony."

I walked up the stairs with Josie by my side. I looked around, admiring the incredible wood work. We reached the bedroom and there was a sliding glass door that opened into the balcony.

"Have a seat," he said, motioning to the empty chair beside his. His lab Jake rose, wagged his tail, and the two dogs sniffed each other's face.

We both said, "Down," at the same time. Josie and Jake complied.

There was silence for a few moments. I noticed Bret watching intently as Teke drove away in her metallic gray Toyota Forerunner. The taillights disappearing around the bend in the road.

"I added this balcony not long after we were married. It gave me a better vantage point to keep an eye on things." He paused before adding, "It still does."

"Thank you for…"

He raised his hand slowly in a halting motion and I knew just as it would be with me if the roles were reversed that he desired no pats on the back or any endearing gratitude. "Care to take a stroll with me?" he asked.

I nodded and stood, as he did. Our dogs followed us downstairs and out into the night. The temperature was already below freezing and our breathing dispensed a vapor like steam into the night air. We walked in complete silence with both dogs heeling by our side until we reached the small cottage that I drove past on the way in.

Bret stopped and studied the old home. He was quiet and I could tell that his thoughts were drifting back to a treasure of stored memories. "My Grandmother, Vicky. This was her home. Let's go inside. I like to check it each day."

We entered the house and I was struck by how neat the furnishings were. Photos hung on the wall and I drifted to one of an obviously young Bret and an older man with the A-Frame house in the background. "My Grandfather. He died soon after that photo was taken. He taught me how to build. How to see something in your mind and shape the wood to fit it."

"Was he better than you?" I asked.

"Far better." He paused for several moments. "I know it's not practical to just leave it here unattended. But I can't sell or rent it and I can't tear it down. She died in this house long ago. The night she died she told me early that morning that it would prove to be her last day this side of Heaven. By then, I knew enough to know she would be right." Chuckling softly, he added, "She always was. She was surrounded by people she loved. Teke was her nurse the last several months. My brother, Alex, Teke's brother, Money, my best friend, and their dad were all here in the end. She looked up at all of us and said, 'don't y'all fret none. We will all be together again one day."

I felt honored that he felt at ease enough to share the narrative of his family with me. My eyes teared but I forced them away. I felt his strong hand on my shoulder. He gripped it tightly and said, "You'll be with your wife again and I can't imagine the pain you have lived in but you still have some living to do. God didn't bring that little girl to your door step without good reason. He knew you were the right man for the job. I don't know why I felt so compelled to show up at your home one day and lend a hand building your cabin but God did. He wanted us connected and he knew you would need some help one day. We are your help."

I nodded my head softly. We walked back outside into the bracing night air.

***

Teke

Jasmin had not spoken as we neared the little shop that sat alone by the highway. I drove to the back of the store and parked beside my friend's red SUV. We got out and the back door to the shop opened.

Once inside, I touched the shoulder of the lady and turned to Jasmin. "This is my friend Kim Sloan, and before you ask, she knows who you are and you can trust her."

"Hi, Miss Sloan," Jasmin said.

Kim was in her early fifties, attractive, with shoulder length light brown hair with a couple of streaks of gray. She had a perpetual smile—the product of a generous heart that I always found so warm, so endearing. She was the real deal. A true southern lady full of charm, grace and good will for her neighbors. We met at the church that we still attended together and became good friends seemingly within minutes of our initial introduction.

She wore a dress with long sleeves. The body of it royal blue and white and the sleeves black. There was a royal blue necklace that matched the color in her dress and a smaller necklace with a simple silver cross.

Kim knelt down to Jasmin and said, "How about we not be quite so formal? Miss Kim sounds better don't you think?"

"Miss Kim," Jasmin responded.

"Young lady. The store is closed. All the blinds are down and no one is here but us so let's walk over to the section with your sizes and you pick out whatever you want."

"I know my sizes."

"Well, off you go little one. Teke and I'll just jabber like girlfriends do and you holler if you need some help. Take your time. My husband, Gary is away at a hunting camp, so I've got nowhere else to be."

We sat on a huge, comfortable brown leather couch that was in the center of the store and watched her as we chatted. "Very practical," I whispered, as we observed her going to the underwear section first.

Minutes later Jasmin returned with two pair of underwear, pants and shirts, along with one set of pajamas.

Kim stood quickly. Oh no, child. We can do better than that."
Kim walked back to the area Jasmin had been at and returned with
an armload of clothing. "Now, see that door to your right? That's
the dressing room. You take your time and try them on and make
sure everything fits."

Jasmin stood silently for several moments. Kim smiled and softly
said, "Jasmin, be a good girl and do like I asked. Everything is
going to be okay," she said, as she winked.

Jasmin spent the next twenty minutes trying the clothes on. She
emerged in khaki pants and a long sleeve navy blue tee shirt. "May
I wear these now?"

"Yes," Kim answered.

"Let me put all these clothes in bags for you." She took two steps
before turning back. "What am I thinking? You see that section over
there? she said as she pointed. "Pick out one of those hoodies that
will fit you. You need something warm for this time of year."

Jasmin returned a few minutes later with a dark green hoodie.

"I have a little beauty room in the back," Kim said. "I can change
your hair style so you don't look so much like the girl on the posters
and on the news."

"That would be good. What will you do?" Jasmin inquired.

"Full-fledged afro."

Jasmin was quiet for a few moments. "But you're white."

Kim erupted in laughter. "Well, yes I am." She chuckled again.
"Who do you think does Miss Teke's hair?"

Jasmin looked toward me curiously and responded, "But she
does not have an afro."

"At one time she did and who do you think did her hair?" Kim
stated.

Jasmin softly nodded and followed Kim to the back room.

The hairdo turned out to be a big hit with all of us. We walked to
the check out area. Kim reached behind the counter and gave me
another bag. It contained gloves, a toboggan and warm socks.

"Thank you so much," I replied, opening my wallet.

"Oh, no you don't. This one is on God and me."

I shook my head softly and I knew that I would never win this argument with my friend. We hugged each other, as I whispered in her ear, "Thank you, my dear friend."

Jasmin stepped in front of Kim and stretched out her hand. "Thank you."

Kim got down on her knees and turned her head slightly. "Can't you do better than that?" She opened her arms and Jasmin walked into them. Kim hugged her and rested her right hand on Jasmin's head for several moments. I smiled as I knew that my friend was praying over this little one who so desperately needed it.

"Let me set the alarm and we will walk out together." Kim looked at the video that showed the parking lot out back. Seeing nothing, she pushed the numbers to set the alarm.

We walked outside, Kim and I both scanning the parking lot. "Thank you again," I offered.

"No worries and if you need more than clothes you have my number. Now get that little one in that vehicle before someone sees her."

***

Clint

Bret and I sat on the balcony enjoying a cup of decaf coffee when I saw headlights bounce through the trees.

"It appears as if they are through with the shopping excursion."

"No," he said in a low focused voice as he continued to study the road. "Headlights are too high."

Another minute passes and a Dodge Pick-Up Truck with slightly jacked up wheels stopped below us. There were two men sitting in the truck, observing the area, unaware that they were being watched as well.

They opened the door and quietly got out. They were to the front of the truck when Bret blinded them with a high-powered flash light. They staggered momentarily, temporally blinded.

"Hey, you want to turn that thing off?" The driver requested with an agitated tone.

Bret kept it aimed at them. "You want to explain what you're doing on my property?"

They were silent as they struggled for the right dishonest answer. Bret decided to assist them. "Don't bother with a lie about taking a wrong turn. You guys drove here to case the house in hopes that no one is home."

"Aw man, we were not casing anything," the other man said.

"Then why are you here?"

They looked at each other and decided it best to just get back in the truck.

They were opening the door when Bret said, "There are a number of reasons why you should not come back and try this stunt again. One is that I have a shot gun pointed at you right now and I won't miss."

I look in his hands and wondered where the shotgun came from. I assume he had it in the corner within reach the entire time. Right now, I thought that if I look up the word smooth in the dictionary it just might have a photo of Bret Marin beside it.

"Another good reason is that currently you're on video from my security system. I'll let the Sherriff view it."

They turned around in the drive and quickly drove away.

Bret already has his cell phone in hand. He spoke to the phone. "Call Teke."

She answered right away.

"Where are you?"

"Approaching our road. What's wrong?"

I smiled thinking about how when you have been in love with the same person for many years that each tone is recognized. Bret sounded as composed to me as any other occasion but his wife had obviously picked up on a slight bit of unease in his voice.

"Drive to the little church. Park behind it and shut the lights off. We are on the way."

"Is this about…" she stammered, not wanting to frighten Jasmin.

Bret was already moving down the stairs and I followed behind him. "No. Couple of guys casing our house. They are in a dark gray Dodge Truck. I ran them off but I don't want you girls running into them on our road. See you in less than five."

He ended the call and told Jake to stay. "You drive," he said to me. Josie heeled by my side without a command. I started my truck and took off quickly down the road. We were fifty yards from the highway when he said, "Take a right at the end of the drive."

Three minutes later I saw the little brick church on the left. I looked toward him and he nodded his head. I drove around back and saw Teke's vehicle. He placed the shot gun between us.

Teke was out of the car now with Jasmin and walking toward Bret. I noticed his outside hand move in a calming downward motion. Teke's nod is barely perceptible.

I find myself walking a little quicker to Jasmin. I hugged her tightly and held her for several moments. "Did someone come after me?" she asked.

I released my hold on her and backed away keeping my hands on her arms. Shaking my head, I said, "No."

"Promise?"

I nodded again.

"Even if you think it's for my own good you have to always tell me the truth."

I breathed deeply at this little one that I felt so compelled to protect.

"Say it."

I chuckled softly. "I promise to always be truthful with you."

She removed the hood and asked with a beaming smile. "What do you think?" as she touched her hair.

Her afro made her even more beautiful. "I love it," I said, with a hearty laugh.

"Miss Kim said it would make me look different than those pictures."

I smiled and nodded. "Miss Kim is correct."

"I have a bunch of new clothes too."

Teke and Jasmin retrieved the bags of clothes and put them in my truck.

"Be careful. Call if you need anything," Bret stated firmly.

I shook his hand. "Thank you. Thank you both," I added, looking to Teke. She moved in for a hug. "My wife would have loved you."

She let go of me and asked, "Why?"

"For one thing you're both huggers," I said, with a slight chuckle. Pausing, I then added, "and the warmth that so easily exudes from you. She carried that same tenderness."

"Take care of my little friend," she responded.

I smiled and we got in my truck and began the drive home. I wondered at what point Bret was able to remove his shot gun from my vehicle without anyone noticing.

Eight
Clint

The insomnia that inundated me nearly every night since Allie departed proved even crueler last night. I watched television until almost five a.m. before drifting off to sleep.

I did see a clip on one of the major networks during my sleeplessness that featured Charlie Rind. He stated that he knew in his heart that she had not perished. I wondered if he really believed this, but he did come across as quite earnest. But he's a politician and if their lips are moving, they are more than likely speaking in lies or half-truths. I love it when a reporter asks any of them a question that requires a yes or no answer. They will pontificate for five minutes and never really address the question.

Could it really be possible that he knew nothing of the abuse his wife committed against these children? It's hard for me to imagine that but like most people I'm basing my thoughts on what I know best, which is that Allie and I shared all aspects of our lives. We hid nothing.

And as I dissect their family-I am reminded of the reality that I have two sons that refuse to speak to me. Life sure can prove to be a muddled disarray of chaos at times.

On the drive home from Jasmin's shopping adventure she asked if she could live with me. I have to confess that I have not devised a strategy of how to accomplish such a feat.

Live with me? I shook my head at the thought. Was there any court that was going to grant custody of a small black child to an old white man? That was not even my priority. I was just hoping not to spend my last years incarcerated for keeping a little girl that I have no rights to.

I searched for answers, finding none that might placate me. I couldn't imagine what an attorney would charge if I was arrested. Allie and I lived a frugal lifestyle. It's not as if we had much choice based on our income. Our bank accounts took a major blow paying for the out of pocket expenses brought on by her cancer, but I would have spent it all and borrowed if need be. Perhaps that was one of the reasons she wanted to come home.

People romanticize love based on so many inerrant beliefs. Authentic love, not the idealistic love scenes displayed on movie screens, is when you live your life placing your spouse and their needs, above your own. And you do it to gain nothing for yourself. You do it simply because their needs are of the greater significance. And if you are really blessed they do the same thing in return.

After selling the house at Carolina Beach and building the log cabin, I emerged with a few thousand dollars. It was certainly not enough to hire the high-profile attorney I would require if I were arrested.

At some point during my fractured time of sleep- I saw Allie clearly in a dream. She wore jeans and a gray and black flannel shirt. I was standing in a lush green valley gazing up at the mountain in front of me. I sensed something to my right and when I turned, she was walking lightly toward me. I watched, unable to move, fearing she would vanish once again.

She stood in front of me now with a stern look etched upon her beautiful face. Closing her eyes, she shook her head. I knew that look far too well. I had done something wrong.

"When are you going to learn, my precious husband? All these needless steps you have kept yourself awake over."

"I have to find a way," I interjected.

"Too much you and not enough him," she said, as she pointed to the top of the mountain. I saw nothing but blue skies and ominous clouds lurking.

"We have been through this before. Trouble appears on your door step and what is our first reaction?" she asked.

"There's no our, anymore. It's just me. A broken-down old man, with little hope or faith left without you."

She closed her eyes and breathed deeply.

"Don't tell me it's still us or something corny like we are always together. I wake alone. I go to bed alone. Every waking moment is an insufferable solitude without you."

I looked up to the mountain and the sky was now a bright color of teal and the clouds were a magnificent white. There is the most spectacular double rainbow that I have ever witnessed.

I see figures on top of the mountain and I don't know how I know this but I am certain that they are angels and they are beckoning for Allie to join them.

"If God brings you to it, he will see you through it. You're that little child's hope."

"Please take me with you," I pleaded.

"What about your little girls? What would become of them?"

"I don't care," I answered tersely.

She smiled and touched my face. "Yes, you do my precious husband." I shook my head and she began to fade from my vision.

I woke with a start. The first thing I noticed was that the room is way too bright for the early morning light that I am accustomed too. The first sound I hear is a sizzling coming from the kitchen. I look at my watch and I am astonished that it's nine thirty.

Rising from the recliner, I see Jasmin in the kitchen frying bacon and Josie is sitting near her feet, watching with ever observant eyes. There are eggs on the counter. Jasmin appears to be as accomplished as any adult at preparing breakfast. She places a K-Cup of Caribou Coffee into the Keurig.

"Good morning," I say. Josie comes to me and rolls over, exposing her belly. I bend down and scratch her for a few seconds.

"I know what I'm doing," Jasmin says. "I won't get hurt or burn the place down."

She removed the bacon from the pan, placing it on top of several paper towels. Switching to another pan she began cracking eggs into it. My coffee was ready and I was about to reach for it when she said, "Go to the bathroom and wash your hands. Everything will be ready soon."

I returned after following her instructions. She gave me a steel gray coffee mug.

"How long have you been up?" I asked.

"Since seven. I took Josie out for her to do her business and before you ask I put her collar on and used the leash. I didn't want to take a chance that she might not listen to me like she does you."

"Very good. Did she give you any trouble?"

"No. She just did her business and we came right back inside. I gave her one scoop of food."

"That's good. Thank you."

"I tried to be quiet since you were asleep. When I woke and came in here, she was laying with you in the recliner. After she went out and ate, she got right back in the chair with you. I thought she might wake you up. She circled on top of you a few times before laying down on your chest. She placed her head under your chin."

I smiled and replied, "She likes to be near me. When I try to sleep in the king size bed in my bedroom, she insists on pressing into to me. If I move during the night and break contact with her, she will wake and move back to a position where she's touching me."

"She was dreaming, twitching for a little while and whimpering and barking under her breath. I didn't know whether to wake her or not," she said.

"She dreams far more than any dog that Allie and I ever had before. Maybe it's her active mind. I don't know."

"Did you ever have a dog like her before?"

"No."

"She behaves so well."

"It wasn't always that way. Cattle dogs are very independent and they want to be in charge. It took a lot of training to get her to behave. There were a couple of times during that first year I was ready to give her back to my friend, Bryan."

She looked at me with a puzzled look and then she smiled. "I don't believe that you would have ever done that and besides, if you had, I would not be here because she would have not been there to save me."

She had a point. "I knew she would be a great dog eventually."

"How?"

"As much as she wanted to be in charge, she knew when I was really upset with her. I think she picked up on a change in my tone of voice or maybe the vibes I gave off."

"What would she do?"

"She had to make up with me at that very moment. She would wag her butt at me and lay down at my feet, or if I was sitting, she would jump in my lap and rub her neck across mine. I told Bryan this and he said, 'You have a good one and even though she resists you at times, she wants you to be the Alpha."

She begins to remove the eggs from the skillet. "Are fried eggs okay? I didn't even ask."

"That's fine."

"Sit at the table," she instructs me.

The breakfast was delicious and I told her so. We were loading the dishwasher when Josie barked and a scant few seconds later the doorbell chimed.

Jasmin disappeared into the bedroom as I moved slowly toward the door, holding my breath as I walked. I detoured to peep out the window and I saw Lori's polar white Mercedes SUV parked in the drive. This was only slightly better than a white and brown patrol car of the Pender County Sheriff's Department.

I opened the door that consisted of antique wood from a log cabin that was torn down in Woolwine, Virginia. It's a small community, in the mountains, not far from the Blue Ridge Parkway. One of my former players, Paul, is part owner and president of a company that specializes in refurbished wood in Davidson, North Carolina. I don't know how he discovered that I was building a log cabin but he called one day as the footers were being poured and said he wanted to send a gift that he thought would be a great addition to the log cabin.

The door was open and now the only thing between us was a full glass storm door. Josie was by my side and she began to growl in a manner I was not accustomed to. I started to settle her but then I thought better of it as Lori backed up a step, with her nervousness apparent on her face. She held a rather large gift bag from Pier One in her hand.

"Stay," I commanded Josie, as I stepped outside and quickly closed the storm door behind me.

The first thing I noticed was that it was quite warm and muggy. The sun was bearing down and the pale blue sky was faultless. Was it just three days ago that it was cold and snowing? The remainder of the snow was thawing rapidly. The surrounding woods sounded like a gentle rain shower.

She was impeccably dressed as always with Abercrombie and Fitch skinny jeans, a bright white top, and a teal blazer, complemented by taupe lace up platform sandals. Her toe nails were painted the exact color of her blazer. The other hand held a Michael Kors purse. The cost of her ensemble probably exceeds the cost of all my clothes combined, especially if you include the purse. "I hope your Christmas, alone, was nice." There was an icy emphasis on the word nice."

The first shot across the bow had been fired.

"Are you going to invite me in?"

At that precise moment, Josie's growl sharpened and increased slightly in volume. Could I love this dog anymore?

"She seems a bit on edge today so I think it prudent to not risk it."

She rolled her eyes slightly and as if speaking to a complete imbecile said, "You could put her in another room."

That was an option. It was not going to happen but an alternative none the less. "I'm not really up for company this morning."

She breathed in deeply. "That's not very polite."

I smiled and replied, "There goes my chance for this year's Miss Congeniality award."

"Is that supposed to be funny?" she asked indignantly.

"I think Josie laughed."

She stared evenly at me for several moments. I worked at remaining expressionless.

She gave me the shopping bag. "I thought these might be a welcome addition to your rustic style," she said, failing to keep the disdain from her tone. "I bought them last week when I was hoping that you would choose to leave this place of desolation and join my family and me for Christmas dinner."

The bag was light and glimpsing into the bag I viewed very colorful throw pillows. I detest throw pillows. I started to inform her that the reason they are called throw pillows is that the first word is throw, as in throw them away but Josie did like to prop her head on the ones that Allie displayed in our home.

"Thank you. You have a nice day." I turned to open the door, holding my palm up, signaling for Josie to stay.

"Did one of your grandkids visit for Christmas?" she asked tersely.

I turned back to her without expression and shook my head.

"I thought that I saw someone with you when you drove past last night, a child."

"No grandchildren," I responded with a smile.

She studied me for a few moments and said, "That's curious." I thought she was about to leave but she continued to stare intently at me for several moments before turning and walking to her vehicle.

I walked back inside. Jasmin detected the trepidation in my expression. "She saw me last night?"

"She knows that she saw someone."

"Will she call that hot line number I saw on the news for anyone who knows about me?"

"I'm not sure but we can't afford to wait to find out. We need a plan."

She took the bag from me with three throw pillows. Love, Peace, and Joy, and each pillow proved a mismatch of gaudy colors. Josie briefly inspected them, as she did all packages.

Jasmin took a second look and stared into the empty bag. She reached in and retrieved the sales receipt. She looked at it and said softly, "I think we need that plan sooner rather than later. This receipt is dated for last night."

I shook my head tightly. "These pillows were no gift. They were a fishing expedition."

Sighing deeply, I slumped into the recliner and leaned back as far as it would go. Knowing something was awry, Josie jumped onto my chest, connecting her neck with mine.

"Could we hide at Bret and Teke's?" Jasmin inquired.

I shook my head. "If we did that they might get in trouble too."

She put her hand on top of mine and then she rubbed Josie. "You could drop me off somewhere and I could call 911. They could come get me and I would make something up about where I have been. I would never tell anyone about Josie and you."

I sat up in the recliner so quickly that Josie fell into my lap. I rubbed her head in apology. Looking at Jasmin, I stated firmly, "No. We're not going to do that."

"What are we going to do?"

I chuckled softly and responded, "I don't know."

I saw questions etched upon her delicate face. The thought of that wicked woman inflicting pain upon her again was something I couldn't bear.

"Jasmin you keep insisting that I be honest with you about everything. The truth is that your foster dad is a powerful man, especially in this region. At the moment, I don't see a way to win but that does not mean I am giving up."

"What do you want?" she asked softly.

"To stay out of jail and to take care of you."

"Do you want me to live with you?"

I could see the concern in her eyes that that she was not sure what my answer would be.

"Is that what you want?"

Her glowing smile warmed my heart. "I want to be part of Josie and your family. I promise that I'll be good."

"I have no doubts about that."

"So?"

"If there is a way that the court system would allow me to be your guardian you can live with us."

She nodded softly and leaned over to hug me. Josie, who never liked to be left out of anything, wiggled her way between us and laid her back to my chest, looking up at Jasmin. We found something to laugh about on a morning, wrought with anxiety.

Nine
Clint

I spent the remainder of the day attempting to formulate a strategy. Each time, I heard a noise, my heart leapt with trepidation that we were about to be surrounded by law enforcement."

I worked some of my stress off by splitting wood, but I couldn't resist glancing at the road to see if unwelcome guests were approaching.

At one point, Jasmin joined me and began to stack the wood as I split it. I thought to tell her to remain inside but to what end? If they came for me, they would take her with them.

It's not as if I didn't know from the beginning that she couldn't hide here indefinitely. At some point, I had to take her to the authorities. I had to hope they might believe us and not return her to the Rind family. If I did that, I could at least afford to hire an attorney to go with me. If I waited until they arrested me, I might be forced to rely on a court appointed attorney.

Josie lay on the front porch with keen observation. Typically, she would at least sniff around before coming back to me but it was as if she were fearful to allow me out of her sight.

First things first. I had to make sure she would be cared for. "Jasmin, will you do something for me?"

"Sure."

"There is a container with Josie's name on it in the pantry. It contains her medicines. Take it to the kitchen table and get a large Ziploc bag and put an assortment of her favorite treats in the container."

Her expression was grim. I shook my head tightly. "Please don't ask me any questions right now. Just do as I ask."

She walked by Josie and went inside. I sat on the porch next to Josie. She laid her head on my leg. As I was rubbing her head gently, I was reminded of how Allie always said to her, "I love your pie shaped head."

Tears welled up in my eyes, rolled down my cheek, and landed on her nose as I realized I had to find her a home, at least temporally. I remembered Allie always said, Josie would never do well being boarded. She went with us on trips to the mountains when Allie was still well. Josie looked up at me as if she knew, and I tell you at that moment, knowing what I had to do, I thought my heart would rupture.

By eight o'clock that evening no one had come for us. I lifted the box containing Josie's items and walked them to the truck. I returned to the cabin and retrieved a bag of dog food that had not yet been opened. "Time to go, Jasmin."

"Where are we going?"

"To see a friend."

"She's not coming back with us, is she?"

I shook my head.

"You can't do that."

"I don't want to talk about it. Please, just get in the truck," I replied wearingly.

Those haunting dark eyes lingered on me for several moments, before she abided with my request.

We didn't speak for the several minutes it took to reach the Marin house. Josie laid her head on my leg a little tighter and closer than usual. Ominous thoughts filled my head, and I speculated as to why it had to be me in this predicament. Right now, I wished that God had found someone else to save this little one. I had to part with Josie and I feared that it would break her heart and perhaps mine as well in the process.

It took everything in me not to break down driving on the gravel road that led to their place. I knew as the hum of the truck motor interrupted the still night that Bret was already on lookout. Soon the headlights from my truck would reach his eyes. I doubted they received visitors this time of night. I started to call Bret first but when everything goes down, they would be checking my phone to see who I had called. I silently prayed that I had not already involved them to the point that would bring law enforcement to their door.

I parked the truck, shut the engine off, and got out, as Jasmin did. I patted my left hip to keep Josie on heal. She was not there. Turning back, I discovered her lying on the seat, not willing to move. She had her front paws stretched straight out in front of her. Her head buried sadly between them.

Closing my eyes, I stood there broken, and I could hear nothing but the sound of my breathing.

"Is Josie okay?" I heard Bret's voice from the bedroom balcony.

"Just her heart," I mumbled before I slumped to the ground in despair. I felt so weak at this moment, the very moment when I needed to be so strong.

It was Teke who reached me first. She held me, patted my back, and rocked me like a small child. There was something missing and I looked up into the truck and Josie had not moved. It was so unlike her not to move quickly to me during any time of distress. I believe that she knew beyond the shadow of a doubt that I planned to leave her here.

Bret was here now and I held my hands up toward him and he assisted me to my feet. "I was going to ask you to keep her with all that is going on. There are events that have ensued that lead me to believe that they are going to know that Jasmin is alive and with me. I just wanted a safe place for Josie. But I can't do it. If I leave her here, she will think I abandoned her and I can't take that."

I stepped to the truck and put my face down on top of her head. "Okay, girl. You win. We will figure something out." As I lifted my head slowly, she raised her own and began to lick my tears.

"Let's go inside and see if these good people can assist us with a plan." This time she responded when I patted my left hip.

The evening was still warm and we decided to sit on the porch. Sinking back into the Adirondack chairs that I assumed Bret built-I studied the lights on their pier that gave off a soft glow. I shared the details of Lori's visit.

No one spoke for several minutes. Jasmin sat like an adult and was silent as well. There was no need to shelter her from any plans. Sadly, she had been forced into this adult world far too abruptly. Jake had his head buried in Bret's lap and was enjoying Bret rubbing his head. Josie had forgiven me but she was still rattled. She jumped into my lap the moment I sat down and curled up in a tight ball. I gently grasped her ear, pulling it repeatedly from the base to the tip. It was something I discovered long ago that she not only loved but it seemed to calm her as well during those challenging puppy months.

"It would appear that I am going to need a really good attorney. One I can afford."

Bret was fixated on the river the entire time. "Be good to get out in front of this the best you can. You hire an attorney and go to them before they come to you. I think the best you can hope for is that you don't get arrested and they place Jasmin in foster care and not turn her back over to the Rind family."

"Jasmin wants to live with us and that's what I desire as well."

"That's not happening overnight. It will be a difficult battle for certain." He turned to his wife and softly said, "Please go inside and type a document that states that in the event that anything prevents Clint from taking care of Josie, we are to be her guardians. Two copies, notarized. Hopefully, we can have something more legally binding before anything goes down. But in the interim, this should help. Clint, place that document somewhere in your home that's very visible. I would suggest on the inside of the front door. I'll have the other copy and hopefully you'll have enough warning to contact me." He paused before asking, "She has a crate, right?"

"In my bedroom, though I hardly use it any longer."

"You live on the end of the street. If you hear any sound coming your way, put her in the crate and send me a 911 text. I'll be at your place quickly, armed with that document. I need a key to your house."

I removed my key from the ring and gave it to him. I had a spare one hidden outside.

Teke was back and she gave me the documents. I perused them quickly and signed. "Where are you going to get these notarized?"

"My friend Kim is a notary and is meeting me at her store. I called while I was inside. Her husband, Gary is driving her over right now."

"I would hate for anyone to get in trouble and if you know Jasmin's whereabouts, which you do, that would place you in a precarious position," I said.

"I'm not concerned," Bret said. "Sometimes, you just have to do what's right and let the chips fall where they may."

"Teke, I'm sure that Clint brought things for his dog. Please move them to my truck and maybe that cattle dog won't surmise that they are missing. That way we will have them if need be. I think that might be what spooked her about coming here."

Teke bent down and kissed Bret on the cheek.

"Be careful," he said.

She nodded her head slightly.

"Take Jake with you," he added.

She called him as she made her way toward Bret's truck. Jake bounded quickly after her.

"Do you need any of the items that you brought for Josie? "Bret asked.

"No. I have plenty of food. That's a new bag. The box has an extra collar and a leash. As well as her medicine for fleas, ticks, and heartworms. She's not due to take the meds for two weeks. I also have a list of all her information you might need. Food amounts, her vet. Probably more information than you'll need."

"I know you're worried about Josie. I give you my word that I'll do everything in my power to bring her home with us, one way or the other, until you make it back home." He paused for a few moments, before adding, "I know an attorney that I have been thinking about calling. I will call him tonight. I am not sure how soon he can be here, but when he arrives, I think you should turn yourself and Jasmin in."

"Is he good?"

"Better than good."

"If I have to sell my home to pay for an attorney there won't be much left to raise this little girl."

"You're not selling your home. And the Lord has been quite generous with us and we can help."

"I can't ask you for that."

"I had a little brother a long time ago and I would have stopped at nothing to protect him. I gained custody of him when he was her age," he said, motioning with his head toward Jasmin.

"How in the world?"

"I had help and I was young enough to think I could take on the world and win."

"Neither one of us are that young anymore."

Bret smiled and moved his hand through his hair. "Speak for yourself." He was quiet for a moment. "We don't have to figure this out tonight. Not all of it. We have a plan in place for Josie and hopefully she won't bite me if I have to get her out of the kennel."

"She won't but I am concerned as to what she might do if the police take me away. If one of those officers is rough with me, she will protect me and they might shoot her. That's the main reason I wanted to leave her here."

"Keep her in the kennel as much as you can. Be very careful when you let her out." He paused and I saw his face tighten with concern. "I'm going to tell you something that you have to do."

I waited for him to continue. "If the police try to question you, say nothing except that your attorney is on the way. Do not allow yourself to be baited into any kind of conversation. If they are nice to you, remain silent. If they accuse you of kidnapping Jasmin, say nothing. If they call you names, do not respond. Are we clear?"

I nodded my head in agreement.

"Nothing, you understand, not a word."

"Nothing," I repeated.

Later as I drove home with the dog I tried to place elsewhere for her own safety and the little girl who wanted to live with me; I prayed there would be no cops on the road to our house. There were none.

That would all change in the morning.

Part Three
Ten
Alex

It was past ten when my phone vibrated and my first inclination was to ignore it. Our two college kids were upstairs in their bedrooms and my wife, Linda, was resting beside me in our dual recliner. We were both reading novels. We did this a lot in the evening after dinner. We both love to read.

I reached for my phone that was resting on the small oak end table that once resided in my Grandmother Vicky's home. I saw the words, Big Brother displayed, and I smiled.

"Hey, big brother."

"I need your help, Alex," Bret stated brusquely.

"Name it."

"It's a long story."

"I got time."

"Do you have to work tomorrow?" Bret inquired.

"No, we shut down the office till after the first of the year. You know that I don't pack my schedule too tightly. I was taught a long time ago by our grandmother that there was more to life than just making money. Now what is on your mind?"

Bret filled him in on the events.

We enjoy a good life, nestled here in our farm house, in the small town of Lansing, North Carolina, just outside of West Jefferson, where my law office is located. My practice has proven quite successful and if I were more driven, it would be even more so. As a young lad, I had witnessed what a special marriage looked like with Bret and Teke. My brother chose not to work seventy hours a week like our father had. Money was nice but Linda and I cared more about our time together with family.

A fading image of my father, Walker Marin, appeared for the first time in quite a while. The last time I saw him I was ten years old. That was when Bret managed to find a way to rescue us from his ironclad grip. He could have gone away without me but he refused to depart without taking his gimpy leg, little brother with him. No one beat Walker Marin, until that day an eighteen-year-old young man and the greatest brother one could ever hope for did just that. Walker Sr. died of a heart attack, a few years later, appropriately in a courtroom while arguing a case. Our two older brothers Walker Jr. and Wally never contacted either of us and that was fine. They received all of the inheritance, but I won the greater prize because I went with my big brother.

He needs me right now and that's a wonderful feeling. The brother that raised me and showed me what a true dad was all about. I hope that I have done as well with my children. They are good kids and Linda is a great mom. My life turned out pretty darn good for a lame kid who lived under the tyranny of an egomaniac father, who reviled in cruelty much like a sculpture fashioned in clay. Our father never laid a hand on any of his sons as far as I knew. He was far too dignified for that type of behavior. He chose to control, manipulate and wound us all with his words. Two of them tolerated it for the money and all the perks of a country club lifestyle. Bret and I were the lucky ones. We escaped.

I smiled at Linda and my thoughts drifted to the day we met. I had recently passed the bar and had just landed my first job. An older man, Matthew Rhodes, needed a partner in his law firm that I now own. My love affair with the mountains began during the trips Bret, Teke and I took when I was a teenager. Late one afternoon, I was driving on the Blue Ridge Parkway, soaking up the late afternoon, May sunshine. The sun was low, but there was still plenty of light to this day. The sky was unblemished. Passing Elk Mountain Overlook, in the Boone area, I noticed a striking lady clothed in dark blue jeans, a long sleeve white linen shirt, and black high heels. I grinned at the memory of her kicking the flat tire on her sporty Datsun 300ZX with her high heels. I drove to the next overlook area, turned around and drove back to where she was, parked, and got out of the car.

"Can I help you?" I asked, as I walked toward her.

She turned and rendered me a stare that appeared quite lethal. "Do I look as if I need any help?"

"Well actually, I was more concerned for the tire's welfare after witnessing your assault upon it."

She tightened her face for a moment, somewhat concealing her beautiful green eyes and said, "Do you think you're funny?"

"Jury is out on that one."

"Jury. You're too young to be a lawyer. Dressed more like a used car salesman in that suit," she said with a dismissive shake of her head.

I took my coat off and folded it neatly and placed it over the front seat of my car. Rolling up my sleeves, I said, "Open your trunk please."

I was changing the tire when she said, "I didn't want to go out on a date with the guy I was supposed to meet twenty minutes ago for dinner anyway? Stupid fix ups. Stupid men."

Looking up, as I tightened the lug nuts, I asked, "How old are you?"

"Twenty-three, if it's any of your business."

"Awfully young to be so jaded."

"Well you can just kiss my…"

She paused before finishing her elegant statement and I looked at her and interjected, "Or I could just finish changing your tire."

"Are you really an attorney?"

"I recently passed the bar and I'm going to work next week in West Jefferson."

"I live in Blowing Rock."

"I don't have a home yet."

"That's great. A homeless attorney."

"I'm renting a log cabin between West Jefferson and Lansing for a few days and I have appointments with the realtor in the morning."

"Are you married?"

I held my bare left hand up for her to see.

"Men take them off when it suits their purpose."

"Not this man."

"Hmmm."

"Again, very young to be so jaded."

She became quiet as she observed me changing the tire. I certainly couldn't work with my hands the way my brother could but thanks to him I have learned the basic things in life. "The spare tire is a little low. Don't drive too far without adding some air."

She nodded her head.

I was walking back to my car when I abruptly turned. "Why don't you have dinner with me?"

She tightened her eyes again and several moments passed before she asked. "Where?"

"No clue. I'm not from here. You tell me."

"There's a nice little place just off the next exit. We can eat on the outdoor deck that's perfect for watching the sunset." She opened her car door and turned back to me and said, "And try to keep up."

I smiled my reply. I'm far chattier than my brother but that didn't mean I failed to recognize the value of reticence. Try to keep up became an oft repeated line of endearment, mixed in with sarcasm, through our years together.

"Where are you from?" she asked.

"Wilmington area." I knew she was scrutinizing me and I was doing likewise to her. She wore her long strawberry blonde hair down and kept playing with it, pulling it up and bunching it on top of her head and allowing it to fall. She was fair skinned and there were a few discreet freckles and she was slightly taller than me with the aid of those tire kicking heels.

"I guess the least I can do is buy you dinner since you changed my tire." Gazing at his right sleeve she noticed a dark smudge from his labor. "I don't suppose that you have an extra shirt?"

"I'll put my coat back on."

"Dinner, huh?"

"Only if you tell me your name."

She eyed me suspiciously. "A man needs to have certain standards," I said.

She allowed a slight smile to escape on that one. "Linda Brown."

"Alex Marin," I said, extending my hand.

She shook it firmly.

Later that night I called Bret and said, "I just met my wife today."

"Does she know it yet?" he asked.

"She will big brother. She will."

The thought brought a smile to my face, and I leaned over and kissed Linda softly on the lips.

"Something on your mind?"

"Can you take the kids skiing without me?"

"If you have a good reason."

"Bret needs me."

"That's a good reason," she responded without debate.

"Will they be disappointed in me?" I asked.

"Disappointed that you can't go, yes. Disappointed in you, never. When are you leaving?"

"The sooner the better."

"Why the emergency? Are Bret and Teke okay?"

"Yes. You recall the little girl that disappeared on Christmas Day?"

"Yes."

I explained the situation to her.

"The little girl is the same age you were when Bret saved you."

I nodded solemnly.

"What time in the morning do you need to leave?" she asked.

"Actually…"

"No," she stated firmly with no room for debate. "You're not leaving now with no sleep and driving all night. That's not happening on my watch."

"They may arrest this man in the morning and take the little girl and give her back to the Rind family. I can't allow that to happen."

"I suggest you go and pack your clothes. I'll make a pot of coffee and throw some things together for the trip."

"You're going with me?"

"You're not leaving in the middle of the night without me. I'm the night owl so I'll drive the first leg while you sleep."

"What about the ski trip?"

"They can go without us. They're not little kids any longer."

I wanted to convince her that I would be fine, but my adamant, take no prisoners wife would not take no for an answer. As it's with a lawyer—it's in life. Do not enter the fracas that you have no chance of emerging victorious.

She leaned in and kissed me and gazed at me with those magnificent eyes and said, "Try to keep up."

I walked away and began to pack.

We were on the road in twenty minutes. Even though it was late, I called an attorney friend, Wylene, who owed me a favor. Years ago, she had a friend who was out of the country when her high school son decided to take an unauthorized ski trip to Boone. Even better, he was busted with an ounce of marijuana. Someone referred me, and I managed to negotiate the plea down to community service, with the understanding that if the kid kept his nose clean, that when he turned eighteen the charge would be expunged. The kid learned his lesson and stayed out of trouble from that time on.

He eventually went to work for Wylene's husband, Bob, as a salesman, upon graduating from UNC-Wilmington. He still holds that position to this day.

Wylene Booth McDonald resided in Wrightsville Beach with her husband. He owned a lumber business in Fayetteville and she was a hard charging, take no prisoners attorney. Once invested in a fight, there was no backing off.

"Wake up sleepy head."

I rubbed my eyes and was shocked to discover that the sun was leaking the first light of the day and that the A frame house that would always be home, stood majestically in front of me. "You drove the entire way?"

"Either that or it was a magic trip. You decide genius."

"You have to be exhausted. I thought we were going to take shifts."

"You were snoring so hard for most of the trip that I thought you might need the rest. Besides, you have a pretty big day in front of you."

I leaned in and kissed her, smelling the coffee she had used for fuel to remain awake. I should have known that if I fell asleep, she would drive the entire way.

"You guys come all this way to make out in my driveway?"

The familiar sound of my brother's voice caused me to chuckle. Linda said as we got out of our white Toyota Forerunner, "Not right now as I had to drive this little brother of yours to your doorstep." She paused, before adding, "But maybe later. Not that it concerns you."

My brother and wife have always gone back and forth at each other quite a bit. I think it began because Linda knew what an influence Bret had on me and she wanted to make sure that it didn't creep into our marriage. She often took on battles that were not yet formed as if she could head them off. She had no worries with my brother. All he has ever desired for me was to be happy. But as it's with most things in life, the foundation something begins with is not easily shaken and neither means any harm. It's just their way of communicating with each other.

Linda looked up at Bret, who stood on the balcony outside the bedroom with his hands resting on the rail and a slight smile etched on his face. He was already dressed for the day, wearing blue jeans and a gray and white flannel shirt. I could see the steam rising from the coffee contained in his black mug.

"You could leave your perch and help with our bags," Linda stated deliberately.

"I would not want to demean one of those strong independent females such as yourself," Bret answered.

Teke was by our car now and Jake barked a muffled greeting. "You two stop right now." She hugged Linda fiercely and then made her way to me. I saw the tears form but not release as she hugged me and kissed me on the forehead several times. I have no memories remaining of my mom who died when I was little. I was ten years old when I met Teke, who was seventeen. What are the chances that a shattered little white boy, living on the fringe of the Deep South, would find a young black woman who would love and raise him like he was her own flesh and blood?

We made our way around to the river side of the house. My brother stood tall and sturdy as always. I smiled and I don't care how corny it sounds for a man of my age to make this statement. But he's my hero. It has been that way for my entire life and it will always be so.

We embraced and held each other strongly without words. When he let go, he cupped my face with his strong hands and looked intently in my eyes. "Thank you for coming, Alex. I hope that I have not got you into a big mess."

He turned to Linda and said, "Thank you for breaking away from your holiday plans."

"Well the golden brother calls, you have to go right?"

Bret nodded in her direction. "I remember the day he called to inform me that he had met his wife. There was such an adolescent appeal in his declaration."

Linda cleared her throat and responded, "He talked about you so much when we first met, and he still does. He was fortunate to have you to save him," she said, in a voice, chalked with tender emotion.

"I always believed that I was the fortunate one," Bret replied.

And then we were interrupted by the sound of multiple helicopters, headed north in the direction of Rocky Point.

"Alex, let's go!" Bret yelled. He was already sprinting toward his truck.

Eleven
Clint

Dawn had broken a few minutes prior, as I sat on the bench in the woods, trying to focus on my devotion time but my thoughts as I strived to read my bible were as darting as the flight pattern of a hummingbird. Jasmin was still asleep and safe in the cabin. I left her a note by the coffee machine, as to my whereabouts. I knew she would not miss it since she had decided in our short time together that she was my personal coffee maker. I had taken the liberty while she was sleeping to make a cup in a travel mug. I took another sip and hoped that the caffeine would clear my head.

Would today be my last free day on earth? I believe right now that my wife would be proud of me and I lived for her approval, both in our life together and even now with her no longer by my side. What would transpire with Jasmin if I was taken away? Would they just rubber stamp her return to the Rind family and what horrid retribution might await her by the merciless hand of Althea Rind?

My worries drifted to Josie. Last night, each time I rose for the multiple trips to the bathroom that a man my age requires, she went with me. I knew Bret and Teke would take care of her, and if I was sent to prison for the remainder of my life, I knew they would provide a good home. But I also knew that some dogs attach to their owner in such a way that it does not leave room to bond with another master. I looked through the trees and I see her sitting without movement on the highest part of the bank of the river. Regal is the word that comes to me as I marvel at her beauty. She is perfectly still as she stares intently over the river.

I opened my bible once more to my favorite book. The Psalms. I'm searching for something, anything that might foster my lagging resolve. My eyes fell on a scripture that was highlighted in a fading color of yellow.

Psalm 61:2 *From the end of the earth I'll cry to You, When my heart is overwhelmed; Lead me to the rock that's higher than I.*

I closed it and drank from my coffee once again. "Come here, girl."

Josie turned toward me and then looked back at the river, seemingly hesitant to relinquish her watch.

"Come."

She walked slowly toward me and as she neared, I patted the bench beside me. She jumped up and laid her head across my lap. I rubbed her head and gently pulled on her ears, hoping that it might calm her but she would not be soothed today.

I know there are many people who think we place too much emphasis on dogs in today's culture. That pet ownership requires too much time and is far too expensive. I would say to them that they have missed out on unconditional love. I believe dogs are a measure of God's love for us. Always present, regardless of how acutely our errors prove to be. They forgive so easily and they hold none of our missteps against us.

"Let's go inside. And if I say kennel, you have to move quickly. This can't be a time for you to be stubborn. When they come, they may casually drive to the cabin or they may come with a fury. I don't want anything to harm you in the fracas."

I rose and retrieved my bible and coffee mug. I patted my left thigh for her to follow but she was running to the river and she ignored my command to halt. She resumed her same position on the bluff and stared intently south. It was then that I heard the muffled noise of helicopters. My first thought was that they had resumed the search. My next consideration was quite dire in what it in all probability meant. I tried to process and thought that there's no way they would dispatch helicopters after an old man. The next image to flash in my mind is Lori. I knew in that moment she suspected that

Jasmin was being kept here. Maybe she cared about Jasmin's welfare or maybe she was getting even for my rejection of her romantic overtures. A sophisticated, cultured woman such as Lori, I doubt has heard no very often.

Josie turned and stared at me and in that moment, she looked despondent. We both alerted to the faint sound of Jasmin's voice calling out to me, nearly drowned in the increasing noise of the helicopter. I patted my side and this time Josie ran swiftly to me. There's a beauty in watching her low to the ground body, running swiftly, but I had a dreadful feeling that this morning was about to render circumstances that held no such splendor.

We raced toward Jasmin with purpose. Josie obeyed my heel command, though I could sense she wanted to break from me and run to her. I saw Jasmin and she was smiling broadly as she walked toward us with a cup of coffee in hand. She was so intent on doing good. Serving me coffee. In that moment, I hoped that she would always be someone who wanted to give more than she took, regardless of what transpired today. She was so fixated on bringing me coffee that she was slow to recognize the now deafening sound of the helicopters. Shock instantaneously consumed her face, producing a look of immediate terror. She dropped the coffee mug and it crashed to the ground.

We were twenty feet from her when several camouflaged clad law enforcement officers all seem to spring from the woods at once. One snatched Jasmin quickly as Josie growled viciously. She took off in a determined sprint toward them as I shouted, "No," over and over. The man had a firm hold on Jasmin, who was kicking and screaming at him to let her down. Josie leapt and bit him on his right shoulder. He retaliated by clubbing her in the head with his pistol and she fell harshly to the ground and didn't move again.

I was knocked to the ground by two men, unable to move as they roughly handcuffed me. The man Josie bit pointed his pistol intently at her as she lay on the ground. I couldn't breathe. I was powerless.

I kept waiting to hear his gun explode and end Josie's life, if she was even still alive.

Seconds that seemed like hours passed before another man placed his hand on top of the pistol that was still aimed at Josie. He slowly pushed it down and the man reluctantly holstered his gun.

I was jerked to my feet and they began marching me toward my destination. I heard taunts, laced with profanity, repeatedly calling me a pervert and a child molester. I wanted to dispute these false allegations but I remembered my promise to Bret.

I tried to stop by Josie but they drug me crudely to an unmarked car. I watched as they handed off Jasmin to two female officers. She continued to struggle. Her mouth gaped open in a look of horror. I was in the back seat of the car now. "What about my dog?" I asked

"I hope the bitch is dead." He picked at the torn clothing near his shoulder where she bit him.

"She thought you were hurting Jasmin."

He turned and his venomous face was the color of crimson, as he retorted, "Hurting little girls is what you do and you're going to prison for the remainder of your pathetic life."

I heard the other officer key his mike and inform the helicopter pilots that the suspect was apprehended. FBI helicopter pilots as it turned out.

As I was driven away from my home, the road was filled with law enforcement vehicles. There was a Pender County deputy standing at in the road, protecting the crime scene. On the other side of him was a plethora of every news outlet imaginable. Lori had indeed leaked the information. She was being interviewed by CBS NEWS as we drove by, and she looked at me with disdain.

As we neared the intersection, I saw Bret and another man standing in front of his truck. Bret held his hands out, with palms down. I had performed that same gesture countless times as a coach when trying to persuade a player to remain calm.

I nodded my head gently.

The man beside Bret stepped boldly toward the car and the driver stopped abruptly. Both detectives were cursing about the intrusion and the one that Josie had bitten, placed his hand on his Glock.

The man motioned for the driver to lower his window. He had a business card in his hand and his phone out.

The driver lowered the window and stated briskly, "Move it, moron."

The man smiled as he handed him his business card. "I'm Mr. Hurley's attorney." There was a familiarity about him and I recognized in that moment that this was Alex Marin. Bret's little brother.

"Takes all kinds," the other detective said curtly. The driver looked at the card and said, "You're from West Jefferson area. Long way to come for this pedophile. Must be your specialty."

I saw Bret's shoulders stiffen, as he stepped closer toward the car. Alex put his hand out low and to his side to halt any additional advancement.

"Mr. Hurley," Alex said kindly.

"Clint."

"Clint. Not a word to anyone but me. I'll be there when you're being processed."

I nodded my head in agreement.

"Are you okay? Did they hurt you?"

"I'm okay. They hurt my dog. I'm not sure she's alive."

"What happened to the side of your face?"

I felt the left side of my face. "I think it was scratched up when my face struck the ground."

Alex looked sternly at the detectives. "Let me get this straight- you guys thought it necessary to tackle a man in his seventies?" he asked harshly.

The driver said firmly. "We are going now. Move."

Alex pointed his phone at me and said, "Clint."

I looked up at him as he snapped several photos of me and a few of the officers. "There better not be another mark on him. Are we clear?" Alex stated without room for debate.

Bret spoke next. "Please allow me to check on his dog."

Silence ensued and Bret stared at the men. "It's the least you can do."

The driver cursed under his breath, powered the window up, and drove away without answering.

***

Alex

Bret stated adamantly, "I have to know about his dog. I gave him my word. Figure something out in a hurry Alex or you might have another client."

"Calm down, Bret. Charging in there right now would not be wise. They are convinced that they are dealing with a child predator. We are all going to be perceived as the enemy."

Bret closed his eyes and nodded toward me. He took a few moments and breathed in deeply. "You know you never asked me."

"I didn't need too."

"It's not as if Clint and I are best friends," he responded.

"I trust your instincts. You would not have called me for help if you were not one hundred percent certain that he's innocent."

"Now, that he has been arrested, does that mean you'll represent both of their interests?"

"I could but I don't think that's what is best. I'm going to represent your friend. First things first-we have to get him out of jail. I have an attorney friend who is a real advocate for children. I have not handled child custody cases, simply because I don't want too. Her name is Wylene Booth McDonald and she's really good."

"Will she back down from the power of Charlie Rind? We saw it at work here today. Look at the firepower," he said, as he pointed toward Clint's property. "Two counties, the FBI, and I don't even know what some of the other agencies are."

"She backs down from no one. She nearly died in a boating accident a few years ago. Most people would have. She's a fighter."

"I guess she's expensive if she's that good. Teke and I will pay her fees but don't tell Clint."

"She won't charge anything. This is right up her alley. Taking on anyone that would dare harm a child. Besides, she owes me a favor and I am going to collect on it."

"Josie," Bret said, looking intently at me.

I nodded softly and said in a deliberate manner, "We are going to walk down there. We will leave the car here. They have the road blocked anyway. Bret, you have to allow me to handle this. No matter what they say. Regardless of insults, you have to back off. Bret, for once in your life, you can't take the fight to someone."

"Yeah," he said curtly, as he began to walk again.

"Hey!"

I could see my unaccustomed harsh tone had startled him, as he turned back to face me. "You either listen to me or stay here. I don't have time to argue with you. I need to be at the courthouse as soon as possible. Now, breathe and allow your little brother to take the lead this one time."

Bret closed his eyes and barely nodded his head. "Okay, I hear you."

"Thank you."

We walked in silence for several steps, stopped at the crime scene tape where I spoke to the officer and gave him my business card. I explained that I was Mr. Hurley's attorney and merely wanted to check on the dog. The man disappeared without a word.

A few minutes passed and a man of average height, if not weight approached us. Jake Jenson was the detective in charge of the crime scene. His belly spilled crudely below his belt that fought to hold up his khaki colored cargo pants. He was wearing a dark blue knit shirt. He reeked of nicotine and his face had the scarring of teen age acne. He was probably forty but he looked older than Bret. "What do you clowns want?"

I smiled and responded, "Well this particular clown represents Mr. Hurley."

"Must be a great vocation," Jake answered, with a sanctimonious roll of his eyes.

"I'm not here to debate with you. We want Mr. Hurley's dog."

"Pretty sure that dog is deceased," he said, as he turned to walk away.

"It can't hurt to check then, can it?"

The detective turned back again. "Animal control is on the way."

"Let us have the dog," I said evenly.

"Nope. Dog bit an officer. If the dog is not dead now it will be put down."

"You're judge, jury and executioner, aren't you?"

"Yeah, and you try to get child molesters off. Again, great vocation. Bet the family is really proud of you."

"Yes, actually we are quite proud of him," Bret interjected.

"The detective eyes lit up in recognition. "Marin. Your older brothers have been practicing law in this area for a long time. I have worked some private security for them on a number of occasions."

Bret smiled tightly and responded, "Now speak of a job to be proud of."

"I know all about you," the detective continued undeterred. "You're the one that married that colored gal a long time ago."

I prepared to grab my brother but to my shock all I heard was laughter. "Colored? For real, colored? You just used the word colored. Hey dimwit, it's the twenty first century. Try to keep up."

There was silence for a few moments and I was grateful that my brother had not decked the bigot who stood in front of us. "As much fun as this is for all of us. What about the dog?" I inquired.

"Animal control is on the way and that is the end of the conversation."

Bret started to duck under the tape but I grabbed him by the shoulder. "No."

"What are we going to do?"

I had my phone out and I was quickly making a call.

"Who are you calling?" Bret quickly asked.

"Wylene."

"Why now?"

"She has two great passions. One is children and the other is dogs. She naturally has connections around here that I don't."

We were walking back to Bret's truck. I was leaving a message for Wylene when a blue Ford pickup with animal crates in the back approached. It was Pender County Animal Control. I held a hand out for the driver to stop.

A plump looking middle age lady with hair the color of dark honey and wearing glasses so big they looked left over from the eighties, powered down her window and looked at us with a frown.

I gave her my card. "Please call me and let me know the dog's condition. I would really appreciate it. Hopefully, she's still alive." I smiled at the lady and asked softly, "What will happen to the dog?"

"If the dog is alive, the shelter."

"Not to the vet first."

"No."

"What if the dog requires medical attention?" I inquired.

She raised her eyebrows as if that were a particular scenario she had not thought of. As she was trying to form a response her phone chirped with the sound of crickets.

It was a one-sided conversation. She said hello and bye and that sufficed as her quota of words.

She looked back at us. "If the dog is alive, who is your vet of choice?"

Bret quickly told her.

She started to drive away. "You'll please call and let me know if Josie is alive?" I asked.

She nodded and drove away.

"That changed abruptly," Bret said, with a puzzled expression.

I smiled broadly. "Wylene Booth McDonald? Now let's get moving. I have a client that needs me and Wylene is on the way to the courthouse to visit Jasmin."

"Is she known by all three names? That's kind of like famous murderers," Bret said.

"There's a rumor, that I am certain is just courtroom folklore that she's distant kin of John Wilkes Booth."

"You're kidding."

"No."

"Have you ever asked her?"

"No. There is a legal conference in Boone that is held every two years that I attend. Truthfully, I think Wylene attends for the parties and the chance to stay with her friend, Helen, who lives outside of Blowing Rock.

"I observed her once in action when someone inquired about it. She just threw back her head and said, 'Well, darling, one just never is sure about these matters.' At that point she walked away with purpose in pursuit of a glass of buttery Chardonnay, her beverage of choice. I have a feeling I'll owe her a case of that particular wine after this favor."

"If she can pull off the feat of Clint and Jasmin being together. I'll buy her as many cases as her heart desires," Bret replied emphatically.

"First task is to keep your friend from remaining in jail. There's no time to waste. Drive me to the courthouse. I'll call you when it's time to pick me up."

***

It was past seven that evening when I collapsed in the chair beside my brother on the deck of the home, I was raised in. The good years of my childhood were found here, unlike the first part when I resided in South Oleander, near the Cape Fear Country Club. It had proven to be a long tedious day. The good news, if there was any was that Clint seemed to be holding together pretty well. I had demanded and been granted my wish that my client being held in isolation. Court was officially closed until the day after New Year's. There was no bail established today and I assumed that one would not be set or that it would be set so astronomically high that it would be unattainable.

A dry cold front had moved through the area and the temperature had dropped substantially. The wind was blowing sharply out of the northeast. The sky was crystal clear and the stars were plentiful.

The door opened behind us and I felt the comforting arms of my wife around my neck. She kissed my cheek.

"Tired, Babe?" she asked.

I sighed and nodded my head.

"The little girl? Is she with the Rinds?"

I pursed my lips and replied, "Not yet. Law enforcement was ready to give her back to the Rind family when Wylene charged in and demanded that Social Services be brought in. She informed all of them that she would be acting as Jasmin's attorney and she would like to see her client alone.

"Charlie Rind was having none of that and he began to push his weight around and that was stifled when Wylene stared at Althea and said, "Ask her about the abuse this poor child has suffered. We will not deny that there has been mistreatment but it was not by the hands of Clint Hurley. Lot of back and forth after that but Wylene has a lot of clout with Social Services. The staff member who Wylene notified to meet her agreed that it would be best to investigate the matter before simply surrendering Jasmin to the Rinds."

"How did things go with Jasmin and Wylene?" Bret asked.

"Wylene has a succinct way of cutting through matters. She asked Jasmin if she wanted to go home with the Rinds. Jasmin shook her head and Wylene said, "Little girl, I'm your only chance of that not happening, but you have to tell me everything right now.

"Wylene explained to her that I was your brother and that you had asked me to defend him. And she promised to check on Josie personally."

"So where is Jasmin?"

"Social Services has her."

"Where do you hide the good stuff for special occasions?" Linda asked Bret.

"The Crown Royal?"

"Yes."

"The small cabinet over the fridge. And thank you for helping Teke with dinner."

"No problem."

She returned a few minutes later with two whiskey glasses. "Crown on the rocks with a splash of ginger ale?"

They both nodded. "Thank you," Bret said.

"How old is that bottle I opened?" Linda inquired.

"Why?" Bret asked.

"It had dust on it."

"This is the first drink of the season."

"Let me guess. You don't like brown liquor unless it's cold."

Bret shrugged and replied, "That's correct."

"Alex is the same way. I guess he followed in your footsteps once again."

"I just never had his basketball skills," I said with a slight chuckle.

"But you played tennis at Duke, and I could have never done that," Bret said.

I laughed. "Still coming to my defense?"

"I know that I don't need too."

"Don't stop on my account big bro," I said, with a big smile.

Linda touched my face and departed to help Teke with dinner. It was quiet for a few minutes and I could tell my brother was thinking about something of long ago.

Bret sipped his drink and said, "The operation you had and the rehab that followed, allowing you to walk normal and be able to run and play sports. You seem to grow up so much during that time. The whining was gone and when you had every reason to cry you kept gritting your teeth and working day after day."

We rarely talked about the times when I could not walk without a severe limp. Sports were out of the question and I was picked on at school and by our father and the two oldest brothers.

Bret raised his glass of the amber colored liquor out to me and we touched glasses. "You were as tough or tougher than I ever was."

"I just wanted you to be proud of me," I said softly.

"I have always been proud of you." He sipped his drink and as he looked toward the river, he added softly, "You are my damn hero."

I was startled by his comment and I fought back the tears that were forming. I know there can never be a compliment either before or after this moment that can rival the stirring words offered by my brother.

Minutes passed, before I said, "Thank God for Teke's mom, finding that doctor. There was no hope offered by the medical community in this area."

"How bad was the pain after the surgery?" Bret asked.

"Pretty bad, but I didn't want to say anything. You had sacrificed so much for me."

"You're my brother."

"So were William and Wally."

"In blood only," he replied sharply.

"And you never crossed paths with them?"

146

Bret shook his head. "Not since the day they departed from here when you were ten years old. They got the old man's money when he died. That was the only thing of consequence to them."

"Do you think they ever could change?"

Bret was silent for more than a full minute. "They have so much of the old man's pride. I guess anything is possible, but I can't see them being able to look in the mirror and examine their hearts to see where they might have gone wrong. A lot of people live that way. It's like the guy that has been fired from ten jobs in a row and it was always the supervisor's fault."

Several minutes passed and I looked behind us to make sure no one was coming out. "I bet you never told Teke about the one dream you gave up for all of us."

Bret turned to face me. "What are you talking about?"

"It was right after you beat dad and we were together. Vic Bubas called and offered you more than a chance to walk on the basketball team. He offered you a free ride to play at Duke."

"How did you know that?"

"He called the house and I answered. You were working. I told him when to call back. You never told Teke?"

He shook his head. "There was no need too. I had responsibilities."

"I guess I never asked you about it back then because I was afraid you would leave me. Even after always being there for me."

"You were ten years old. I wasn't going anywhere."

"Not even to play at Duke?" I asked, with a slight shake of my head in dismay.

"Not even to play at Duke."

We both sipped our drink in the stillness of the evening. We heard a slight noise and seconds later three deer walked casually in front of us, disappearing a few seconds later into the darkness. "I was too young to understand all that you did. As I got older it has amazed me to realize all that you did for Teke, for me, for Vicky. You were not far from a kid yourself."

"I had a lot of help," he humbly offered.

"Still."

"Still, I would make the same choice. My life has been richer because of all of you. Basketball, as much as I loved it could not have ever given me anywhere near what I have."

"So, only you and I know about Vic Bubas calling that day."

"Money knows."

"You told him?" I asked.

"He was a big part of the reason that Coach Bubas changed his mind. Duke and State's freshman teams were scrimmaging at Duke and Coach Bubas was watching. He approached Money afterwards and wished him well at State. He had recruited Money hard just like most of the schools that thought they had a shot. In the course of the conversation, Money told him that the best player he ever played against was me and that it was a shame I was not playing. He tried to talk his coach into letting me play at State but they didn't have any scholarships available. Duke had a player that left campus the first week of school and that freed up a scholarship."

There was a pause of several moments. "It's okay. I was never going to be good enough to have an NBA career like Money. I got his sister. That's a prize that far exceeds basketball."

"Both of you came out well. Money played eleven years in the league for the Trailblazers. He works in their front office and he married an Oregon cheerleader."

"I miss him. Teke does too. We both hoped that one day he would return home but he has a great job and his wife is from Portland. Besides, his parents are gone. Somehow, I think it's easier for him to live far away from where his dad lived."

"Clarence was a great dad," I offered.

"Clarence was a great everything. I only wish he could have moved on from loving Teke's mom and found someone to share his life with. When Jacky died a few years ago, he was so quiet for months. We would do a job together but he didn't cut up with me as was typical. It was only work talk for the most part. Teke told me to just keep him working. The year that Teke and I got married they began seeing each other again. It went on like that for a few years before they called it quits again. She loved living in Philly and Clarence was not leaving here."

Bret held his glass up toward the sky. "Maybe they are together now. Like Vicky said when she was near her death. We will all be together one day. One big family. I sure hope she's right."

There was silence once again. The lonesome whistle of a distant train permeated the night.

My phone rang and I answered it quickly. I listened intently and then I thanked the other person and ended the call.

"That was the vet. Josie was unconscious for a long time. She has a concussion and is being monitored closely by staff. She will not be alone tonight and the vet said that she has told her emergency staff person to call her if Josie's condition deteriorates."

"Be good if we could get word to Clint," Bret suggested.

"Hum." I made another call. "Wylene. Can you get word to Clint that Josie is alive? She has a concussion and hopefully she will be okay?"

The call ended and I said, "She will take care of it." I paused before asking, "Clint is the real deal, isn't he?"

Bret merely nodded.

"I watch what that man is going through, but he was more concerned about the welfare of Josie and Jasmin." I paused and deliberated on my next words. "If this case goes to trial, I'll be here for the duration."

"It could take a long time and you have a business of your own," Bret answered.

"I have a good young attorney in my firm. She can handle things in my absence." I drank the last of the remnants in my glass and set it down on the rail. "There's something I want you to know, Bret."

He turned to me.

"I won't lose."

He studied me for several moments. "Lot of politics involved."

"I was born for a case like this. One thing I'll need is to be able to set up a temporary office at Vicky's house and work from there without interruption."

"I think the ole gal would be the first to offer you that."

Linda walked out and took each of our glasses. She returned moments later with fresh drinks. Teke was with her, holding two drinks, and she gave one to Linda as they sat in chairs next to us. "Dinner is ready anytime," Teke said.

Bret smiled and said, "Josie is still with us. She has a concussion. As soon as she's well enough, I'm going to bring her here." He paused, before asking, "Where is Jake?"

"He is lying on the balcony and watching the road like you do."

"You boys have a good time catching up?" Linda asked.

We nodded our heads simultaneously. Bret said, "Talking about the situation but also about how blessed we have been by the people that remain in our lives, and to those that have departed."

I sighed loudly and shook my head. "Pancakes at Clarence's home on Saturday mornings. How awesome was that for a little kid?"

Silence endured for several seconds. "Time for dinner," Teke said.

We all stood together. "How about a toast?" I suggested.

We raised our glasses together. I smiled broadly before proclaiming, "*Hearts have no color.*"

We all clinked our glasses and repeated, "*Hearts have no color.*" We drank in unison.

Twelve
Teke

It was ten o'clock the following morning when Bret asked me to ride with him to visit Josie. We had received no phone calls about her condition and we hoped that was an encouraging sign. Alex departed before the promise of today's sun. He would spend most of the day at Vicky's strategizing and would visit Clint at some point during the day.

"Is Jake going?" I asked.

"Yes."

"Did you call the Vet?"

"No."

"What is it that you're not telling me?" I inquired.

"The detective that Josie bit. He's not the type to let something go. I don't trust him not to try and pick up Josie and deliver her personally to the shelter. This looks bad on paper. Detective performing his job and Josie bites him in the process, though with all the apparel that he was wearing, I doubt Josie even broke the skin."

We were in his truck and driving down the dirt road that led to the highway. Alex's car was in front of Vicky's.

"Have you ever worried about Jake biting anyone?" Bret asked.

"Not at all. He might lick them to death," I responded.

"But if someone tried to hurt us it might prove to be a different story, and that's all Josie was reacting too. Picture it. Two men emerge from the bushes and snatch Jasmin and she's resisting the entire time. Josie should not be punished for that. Her instinct was to save Jasmin."

I nodded my agreement and we rode in silence for the remainder of the drive.

We entered the Vet's office and asked to speak with Dr. Lanier. It was five minutes later when a slim, attractive woman, with brown curly shoulder length hair, who appeared to be in her early fifties, greeted us.

"I have one good news and two bad news to report," she said, after introductions were made. "Josie seems to be recovering from the blow. She will need to take it easy but she's young and should physically recover quickly."

"Physically?" Bret asked.

"She's traumatized. I take it that she's very attached to the owner."

"Very much so," Bret answered.

"She has separation anxiety for certain."

"You said two bad news," I interjected.

"She won't eat and is barely drinking water. I have had her on an IV to keep her hydrated. The kennel is in the back. Walk with me," she said as she began moving briskly.

There was one room with approximately twenty cages. Half contained dogs of various breeds and half were unoccupied.

We continued walking to a separate room. There was only six cages, and only the one at the end of the room facing us, contained a lone dog. Josie. She was lying on her stomach and her paws were stretched out in front of her. Her head was nestled in between them. I was not certain when I had ever witnessed a more pitiful look.

"I thought it best she be in here alone and not around so much noise. And even though she can't tell me, I'm assuming that at the very least she has pain in her head. Staff has tried to coax her to go out this morning but she has remained in the cage in that same position. As you can see, we have even left the door open, in hopes that she might venture out."

"Can we take her with us?" Bret asked. "I have a notarized statement by the owner that he desires that be the case."

"Wylene is a big advocate for dogs in this area. She has already called and informed me of that. I don't think I need to see any letter."

The intercom buzzed and they heard. "Dr. Lanier, There's a call from Detective Ward for you."

"Please don't take that call. At least right now," Bret said.

She nodded and said in a raised voice, "Tell him that I'm busy. I'll get in touch with him later." She looked at us. "Wylene explained what happened. I'll be out of town for a long holiday weekend. I'll tell the staff not to give out my cell number as it pertains to Josie unless you need me. You have until January second, when I'm back at work, before I return that call to the detective. I hope things look better by then. Josie should not be put down for doing what she did."

"Thank you," we said together.

"I will go up front and get some meds for her. I will be back in a few minutes. You have her food, right? I don't want her switching anything right now."

"Her owner brought me her food and her meds," Bret responded.

"Responsible dog owner. My favorite kind." She reached in her lab pocket and gave Bret several treats.

"Responsible person as well and a truly good person. Don't believe what you read or hear on television," I said firmly.

She nodded her head indifferently. She left and I observed as Bret walked slowly to the crate and sat down in front of it on the cold gray cement floor. "Hey, girl. I need you to come home with us and I'm going to believe that it won't be for long. You're a special girl. I knew that right away when I worked on the log cabin. You sure are devoted to him."

Josie's eyes moved up slightly for just a flicker of a moment but she remained transfixed in her position. Bret offered her a treat but she failed to acknowledge it. He touched the top of her head gently and continued to speak softly, encouraging her to come but she refused to budge. Several minutes passed and Dr. Lanier moved so noiselessly that I had not realized until now that she was standing by me, watching.

I saw Bret's face lighten and I knew that he had an idea. He stood and walked to us and he hugged me.

"That poor dog is heartbroken," I said, fighting back tears.

"I know. I want her to come out on her own if possible. Please go to the truck and bring Jake and Josie's leash."

"Who is Jake?" Dr. Lanier asked.

"Jake is our dog-a friend to Josie. I think my husband has an idea worth exploring. I will be back quickly."

I returned with Jake on lead. Bret knelt down, speaking evenly to him, as he removed the lead. "Heel," he said. They walked toward Josie and stopped a few feet in front of the open crate. "Down," Bret commanded and Jake quickly complied.

Bret walked back to Dr. Lanier and me. The three of us watched together and I prayed silently for help. Jake studied Josie for several moments and then he scooted closer to her. I think we were all shocked by what occurred next. Jake laid his head on top of Josie's head and left it there.

The intercom buzzed again. "Detective Ward called again and said he would be here in twenty minutes. I informed him that we were about to close and that you were leaving for the weekend and he demanded that I tell you to wait."

"I'll be up front in a minute, she answered." She turned to us. "I was not aware that Detective Ward could tell us when to close. Still, it's probably a good time for us all to make an exit. Don't worry about my staff. The doors close in five minutes and no one is allowed in, including an ill-mannered detective."

At that moment something miraculous transpired. I gripped Bret's arm. "Look," I said softly. Jake was walking slowly toward us and trailing behind him was Josie. Bret knelt down and rubbed Jake's head. "What a good boy." Turning to me, he held his hand out for Josie's leash. He took it and fastened it to Josie's collar. "Teke, put Jake's leash back on and walk him to the truck. I'll follow behind with Josie."

"Thank you, Dr. Lanier," Bret said, as they reached the front door.

"Thank you so much," we both said to her.

We walked outside to the truck and both dogs climbed into the back seat. On the ride home I looked in the back and Josie was snuggled close to Jake. She closed her eyes and a few moments later she was softly snoring.

Thirteen
Clint

I woke after a fitful two hours of sleep. The first thing I was aware of is the suffocating odors of this horrendous place. The most prolific aroma smells like a concoction of pine oil and bleach.

I know it's still dark outside, even though I had no access to a window. My body clock informed me that it's probably five a.m. The wonderful breakfast that the New Hanover County Jail serves will be available soon. I think I have lost five pounds but it would be much more if my attorney had not brought food during his visits.

Alex is soft spoken, especially for an attorney. He's also kind and humble, but underneath his exterior, I sense a quiet confidence that I find reassuring.

I told him each day that I would find a way to pay him and he tells me that's of no concern. He just wants to see me set free. I asked him the first day why he believed in my innocence.

He smiled broadly. "My brother has never steered me wrong in my entire life."

And while I appreciate his confidence that I'll be set free, in my early morning solitude, I'm overwhelmed with cheerless thoughts. I think of Jasmin and Josie and I wonder how they are. Hopefully, I'll eventually be found innocent of these charges but even if that's the case, what court will surrender a little girl to an old man like me? And while I am grateful that Josie is at the Marin home, she also bit an officer, regardless of how justified it might have been. What if she's euthanized for that act?

I opened my worn bible to Psalm 91, which I have thanks to Alex. The first scripture of this chapter has always been a favorite of mine. *The one who lives under the protection of the most high dwells in the shadow of the almighty.*

"Lord, I surely need to be in your shadow today. It appears that all is against me. You know I did nothing wrong. That might serve as my only comfort in what remains of my life if I'm convicted."

"No. All is not against you."

I looked up at my early morning guest. Alex stood outside my cell with Ken, the one jailer who has not treated me as some guilty pervert.

Ken is around six feet tall, give or take an inch. He's probably close to fifty. His bright eyes and well-groomed beard, remind me somewhat of Tyler Perry.

"I have a suit for you. Ken is going to escort you to the shower and allow you adequate time to get cleaned up and dressed."

"I have a confession to make," I responded.

"That's the wrong word to use in this place, Clint," Ken said.

"My wife always tied my tie. I have not tied my own since we began dating over thirty years. I'm not sure where to begin. I think one of my sons tied it the morning of her funeral."

"Will they be here this morning?" Ken asked.

I shook my head.

Ken opened the cell. "You get cleaned up and ready for court. I'll tie your tie."

"I know you hear this everyday but I didn't do any of the things I was accused of."

He shook his head in tiny shakes, barely moving.

"Ken, is the little diner around the corner open this early for breakfast?" Alex asked.

Ken looked at his watch. "By the time you get there it will be."

"Could I bring you something?"

He paused and thought for a moment before shaking his head.

"You hesitated," Alex, said with a slight smile.

"The country breakfast combo would be great," Ken said, reaching into his pocket.

"Put your money away. Thank you for being kind to my client."

"I get tainted working here and if you saw the stuff I have you might be as well, but at the same time, I try not to assume everyone in here is guilty. My wife watched the news, and she thinks something just does not add up with this story. She can't put her finger on it but I have found she's usually right about such things."

"I had a wife like that," I said.

There was an awkward quiet now. Alex placed a hand on my shoulder. "I'll be back in a few minutes." He smiled at Ken and walked away.

***

I'm reminded of another of my favorite verses as I shuffled into an overflowing courtroom in handcuffs and leg irons. Micah 6:8 *He has shown you, O mortal, what is good. And what does the LORD require of you? To act justly and to love mercy and to walk humbly with your God.* I would say at this humiliating moment that I'm about as humble as a man can be.

Alex stood at the table and waited as my adornments were removed. He smiled as he placed a hand on my shoulder. Bret was seated in the first row behind me. He nodded encouragingly. Alex leaned in so he could be heard over the chatter. "Today is about seeing if we can get a bail that's affordable. It's a long shot but with an agreement to wear an electronic tracking devise on your ankle it might be possible. They may say no bail or in all probability they may set it astronomically high to make a statement."

He looked away for a few moments before turning back to me. "The judge will ask how you wish to plea and you'll answer firmly, not guilty."

"You have told me all of this before. Are you nervous, Alex?"

He smiled and said, "A few butterflies. Just like before a big game, Coach." He studied me for a few moments. "You can't take

158

anything personal that's said here. I know that it will be a challenge. This is a big case and the Assistant District Attorney will certainly play to the cameras. But on the plus side, Wylene says we have a fair judge."

I turned to Bret, who stood and leaned in. "How is Josie?"

"Better. We have Jake to thank for that. He led her to our house and when she refused to eat, he pushed her bowl of food to her. When that failed to work, he began to bark and paw at her. It worked. She slowly began to eat. She's lost a couple of pounds but she will be fine."

"I can't thank you enough."

He shook his head dismissively. There's something I have discovered in my brief friendship with Bret Marin. He can handle about anything tossed his way but praise.

Even though I was certain that there are many eyes on me at this moment I sensed a certain laser like attention directed toward me. Looking toward the district attorney's table, I saw Charlie and Althea Rind seated behind it. Charlie's face is red and he muttered something in my direction. I don't think there were any charitable words offered.

My face was expressionless toward him for a few moments but then I moved my gaze to his wife. I stared intently at the real villain in this courtroom. She was unable to meet my unflinching stare and, in that moment, I sensed that some of her worst fears have come true. Her secret years of abuse might become public knowledge.

Jay Jackson, the Bailiff, stood erect as his baritone voice filled the courtroom. "All rise. The Court of New Hanover County is now in session, the Honorable Judge James T. Willingham presiding." Judge Willingham was tall and lanky with a slight paunch. He was bald with a few noticeable age spots on the front top of his head. He wore gold framed glasses that looked just as he does—as if he might belong to another era. He sat at the bench and the rest of us took our seat.

I heard a rise in the murmurs of the crowd and turned around to see what the commotion was about. Wylene walked with purpose in our direction, though I'm not sure why, as I'm not her client. She was stylishly attired in a dark blue long sleeve dress with matching stiletto heels. The white pearl necklace added a touch that reminded me of photos of movie actresses from the fifties. She may have been nearly sixty years of age but she sure had the attention of every male in the courtroom, including the Judge, though his concern might not be about her exquisite beauty.

She opened the gate that separates the crowd from those of us that are required to be here. She leaned down and whispered to Alex, who nodded his head gently.

"Miss McDonald. Care to inform the court what you're doing at the defense table?"

"Your Honor, if it pleases the court, I'm here to assist Mr. Marin. We have a mutual interest in seeing justice prevail."

"Very well," he said. Wylene thanked him and sat beside Alex.

The Assistant District Attorney, Lynette Strickland, a petite, thirty-year-old blonde stood up. She was good, but too quick on her feet right now. "Judge Willingham. We..."

"Sit down please, Miss Strickland," the judge stated firmly.

She blinked her eyes several times. Several awkward seconds passed as she debated her next move.

"Miss Strickland, you're still standing. Why?" the judge reiterated.

Embarrassed, she sat down with as much dignity as she could muster.

"Now that I have everyone's attention. Since we are not trying this case today, we are not going to be giving any speeches to play to the media. We are here to discuss bail after I read the charges."

A.D.A. Strickland sprang back up to her feet. "Surely, you would not grant bail in a case such as this, Your Honor."

The judge rolled his eyes and softly shook his head. "You apparently have had your morning coffee, Miss Strickland."

A perplexed look consumed her face. "Yes, but I hardly see what that has to do with anything."

"Maybe you should consider switching to decaf."

There was faint laughter in the courtroom as she sat down. Her face, the color of a not quite ripe tomato.

"If there are no more interruptions, I'll read the charges." He did so.

"How do you plea, Mr. Hurley?"

Clint, Alex, and Wylene stood together. "The only thing I'm guilty of is helping a little girl."

"I'll take that as a not guilty. You may sit down."

"Now, Miss Strickland. Your turn has arrived. Speak and be brief."

Slowly, she rose. "We are adamant that no bail be allowed." She glanced at Congressman Rind, nodded her head, and sat down.

Congressman Rind stood. He placed one hand on his wife's shoulder. "Your Honor—"

"You do not have permission to address my courtroom," Judge Willingham, stated firmly.

"That man took our daughter," he said, as he jabbed a finger in my direction. There was an instant murmur of voices in the courtroom.

Judge Willingham stared at the congressman for several moments. "Sit down or I'll have you escorted from this room." Charlie Rind reluctantly sat down.

"We are here to determine bail and not guilt or innocence. I know that in our time of social media and twenty-four-hour news that there is a rush to judgment on everything and everybody wants to give their opinion. But in this courtroom, I try to perform my job fairly. It's something that's lost today in our expediency to be heard. Something even more important that's lost is that Mr. Hurley is actually innocent until proven guilty. I know that's something we say but we really don't mean." He paused for several seconds. "However, in my courtroom, that's how we will operate."

He removed his glasses and wiped them with a cloth, then put them back on and looked in our direction. "Mr. Marin, do you think you can address the court regarding possible bail and not be endeared to giving speeches?"

Alex stood and smiled slightly. "I understand and I request a reasonable bail. This man has ties to this area for his entire life. He has never had so much as a speeding ticket." He sat down.

Alex had told me to expect no bail or a very high bail but I think even he was shocked when we heard the judge say, "Twenty million on bond."

The A.D.A. smiled. "Thank you, Your Honor," she said, as she began to pack things into her a briefcase.

The judge, hearing nothing from my defense table was about to bang his gavel when I heard a voice behind me that I recognized. I turned and was met with a nod and smile from a tall, athletic looking white man, with short brown hair. "We can cover that," he stated to the judge confidently.

"We?" the judge asked.

"I'm not alone."

"Who are you?" the judge demanded.

"Kevin Keen. I played for Coach Hurley the first three years he coached. He told my dad that he wasn't sure if I could walk and chew bubble gum at the same time but he sure did like the fight I had. I'm here today, fighting for my coach and against these ridiculous charges."

The judge studied him for a few moments. "You said that you were not alone. What did you mean by that?"

I saw another man stand. "Kevin Skipper, point guard," he stated, as he held up a legal property document, shook it slightly, and added, "My home. Both my homes to be precise."

Beside him another man stepped out. "Todd Osborne. Skipper needed someone to pass the ball to down in the post." Kevin Skipper shook his head in dismay and smiled hugely. "I'm an underpaid teacher but all I have in this world, I'll put up for Coach's release."

The next man spoke. "David Glenn." He held up his property document. "Coach never would hurt a child, though he sure did make me run sprints one day until I thought I might die." I heard a murmur of soft laughter throughout the courtroom.

I smiled as the next person rose. He still looked like he could play some ball. He was a shade less than six feet tall, sporting a shaved black head, soft sincere eyes and he always looked both very humble and very self-assured at the same time.

"Adrian McCrae."

"And I take it that you played for Mr. Hurley, as well?"

He held his head high and stated firmly," I was the opposition." Some of the players chuckled at his remark. "Actually, arch rivals and Coach Hurley said I use to keep him awake at night, worrying about how to contain me. Of course, Skipper was guarding me, so there was only so much Coach could do." There was more laughter in the courtroom, especially among the former players. "Coach and I always respected each other." He held up a document," and nodded at the judge.

I began to scan the audience for my boys, who were now successful men with their families and their careers. I knew without question that Kevin Keen had spearheaded this show of support. We still got together for lunch a few times each year and he never allows his old ball coach to pay.

Players kept standing one at a time, announcing their name, and offering to cover a portion of my enormous bail. I hear the names, Stephen Wolff, Reggie Mathis, Brad Chapman and Jeff Neher. I bowed my head on to the table and softly began to weep.

These wonderful boys of mine had come to show support and in the process had showed an old ball coach that even though that allusive State Championship that I so coveted had escaped me. I had won so much more than that one game, and regardless of where my remaining years were spent, I knew that I would no longer be haunted by a lucky shot.

Names kept being called and I wondered why the judge didn't intervene and put a halt to what was happening. I raised my head, accepting the handkerchief from my attorney. Two sharply dressed brothers stepped forward together. Lenny Rowell spoke, "My brother Marcus and I own several properties together. They are worth in the neighborhood of four million dollars."

The last one, even though I had not seen him in years, I would have known by his persuasive smile and the perpetual gleam in his eyes.

"Paul Atkinson. Power forward and three-point shot specialist."

I shook my head gently, closed my eyes, and chuckled. Those that played with Paul like Brad Chapman laughed the hardest. Paul was an undersized power forward, who played inside with great grit and determination. He once launched a three-point shot and I removed him from the game and in no uncertain terms, told him I would break his arm if he ever did that again.

He grinned and replied, "Okay, Coach. Back to playing defense, setting picks and grabbing rebounds." His jump shot had a range more suited for the paint and not beyond that but his charm even caused his old coach to chuckle in the moment. As I was laughing at his antics he took that opportunity to check himself back into the game without even asking me. I looked at my assistant coach, Richard Mears, and just shook my head.

Richard said, "Paul being Paul and I wouldn't take anything for him." He paused, before adding, "And neither would you."

I heard Foster's voice next. "My wife, Carol and I own a log cabin on a few acres. I have my deed here," he said, raising it up for the judge to see.

The courtroom was finally still and the judge took the opportunity to ask, "Is that all?"

"No, Your Honor." Bret stood and held his property document up. He remained standing.

"Something else?" Judge Willingham inquired.

"Your Honor, if we are still short of the funds, I have an email from my brother in law, Money Wilkins. It states he will cover the remaining funds if needed."

A.D.A. Strickland quickly stood and declared, "In light of this we reiterate that no bail be granted."

"You can reiterate all you choose but I set the bail amount."

Wylene stood, which I think startled not only me but Alex as well. "Permission Your Honor?"

"Pertaining too?" Judge Willingham asked.

"Something that may persuade you to drop all the charges."

"Better be good."

"I always am," she remarked with a confident smile.

"Proceed, Miss McDonald."

"Social services has Jasmin available to speak with you. She desires to be heard. I know what she wants to say but I have no intention of clouding the issue. I request that you adjourn court for a few minutes and meet with her, Your Honor. Please."

A.D.A. Strickland, still had not retained her earlier lessons on keeping quiet. "Your honor, I..."

And that was as far as she got. "Please be quiet," he stated harshly. He removed his glasses again and began to clean them. The entire courtroom was deathly still. The judge seemed to be in deep thought. Beads of perspiration could be seen on his head. Finally, after a good two minutes, he said "Court is adjourned for fifteen minutes. In my chambers," he said. He banged the gavel, rose quickly and disappeared from the courtroom.

I joined Alex, Wylene and A.D.A. Strickland in the judge's chambers. The door opened and the bailiff led a middle age black lady with wide hips and an all business expression into the room. Trailing behind her was Jasmin. We all sat down at a large deep brown table.

"Who wants to go first?" Judge Willingham asked.

A.D.A. Strickland studied her sensible shoes. Maybe she had decided that she had rankled the judge enough for one morning. Jasmin's escort spoke first in a pleasant southern voice. "My name is Wanda Thomas and I'm with social services. I'm assigned to Jasmin's case. Judge, I have spoken at length with Jasmin and I'll allow her to tell you the details of what has transpired. The only thing that I might add is that Jasmin is not a typical ten-year-old child. Meaning no disrespect, I suggest you not treat her that way. From the time she lost her mom and with what she has endured since, she's as mature or even more so than many adults I deal with." Turning to Jasmin, she smiled, winked and said, "Tell the judge your story sweetie."

Jasmin stood erect and looked the judge right in the eyes. "What should I call you?"

The judge smiled slightly. "You may simply call me judge. Now, proceed with your story."

"It's no story, Judge. It's the truth. Mom taught me to always tell the truth."

The judge nodded and smiled slightly. "Go ahead."

"First thing is that I ran away on Christmas Day. I stole a kayak and took off down the river. Mr. Hurley and Josie saved me when the kayak flipped over."

The judge interrupted at this point. "Who is Josie?"

"Mr. Hurley's dog."

"Okay, please continue."

She proceeded to tell of the events that took place on that day and what had transpired since then. She also told him who the real abuser was.

"Is that all?"

"No sir. Mr. Hurley did nothing but help me. He didn't abuse me, kidnap me or harm me in anyway. I have never known a kinder man."

The judge nodded ever so slightly and watched as she sat down. Wanda patted her shoulder gently.

"Permission, Your Honor," Wylene asked.

He nodded.

She stood and handed him a medical report and also gave one to the A.D.A. Judge Willingham adjusted his glasses and began to scan the paper as Wylene spoke. "The medical report says she has never been sexually assaulted in anyway shape or form by anyone. She has marks on her back and buttocks from physical abuse. But you'll read where the marks are several weeks old. There's no way Mr. Hurley could have caused them. Jasmin has informed you who the real abuser was and that's who should be on trial. I don't care whose wife she may be."

The judge began to speak. "We have us a situation, don't we? I'm going to make a suggestion and everyone in this room will need to agree if we move forward with the conversation I would like to initiate. There will be no problems in the future for any of you that choose to say no. I'm off script here. I would need what is said here to remain here. Jasmin, I would like to begin by asking you a couple of questions. You have already convinced me that you'll answer truthfully."

He removed his glasses and placed them on the table. "How does everyone feel about a civil private conversation? Before you answer, I'm asking all of you to do one thing. Look at Jasmin and let's try to do right by her. Surely that's more important than winning a case."

He waited as the people in the room agreed. A.D.A. Strickland was hesitant. She pursed her lips and audibly blew air out. She rubbed her forehead.

The judge knew that he had been hard on her this morning. He smiled and said, "Miss Strickland. When I say no one is to repeat what is said here that includes me. Now, what you tell your boss later is up to you. Understand? He'll hear no different from me."

She shook her head and exhaled loudly. "In for a penny. In for a pound. Sure, Judge."

He nodded his head gently. "Jasmin, why did Mr. Hurley not call the authorities?"

"Because I begged him not too. I was so afraid of having to go back to the Rind house."

"And Mr. Rind did not know of the abuse?"

"He was away a lot. She was nice to us when he was home. He had no reason to look at my bare back or bottom where she beat me."

"Did she beat all the kids?"

"Not like she did me. I was the defiant one. Her words."

"Why did no one speak up?" the judge asked.

"We were afraid. Some of the places the kids had been fostered at were even worse."

Judge Willingham shook his head and muttered, "Better the devil—"

"Better the devil you know than the devil you don't," Jasmin said. "The older kids said that and so did the housekeeper. I did tell her once. She told Miss Rind. I really got a beating that time. I learned to keep quiet."

"Where were you going on the day you escaped?"

"Wherever that river took me. I think God smiled on me that day. He took me to Mr. Hurley."

"You're an amazing little girl. I want Wanda to take you outside now."

168

Jasmin rose and took a step toward the door. "You're going to let Mr. Clint go home, aren't you, Judge?"

"Let me worry about that."

"I want to live with Josie and him. I know he's older but he has a lot of help. We'll have a lot of support."

"One thing at the time young lady. But I'll tell you this. You're not going home with the Rinds today."

"Your Honor, "Wanda said.

"Yes."

"I'm not saying that Mr. Hurley can adopt Jasmin but for now, assuming you release him, I don't have a problem with placing her with him while we work out where she lives permanently."

"Duly noted. Thank you, Wanda. I know you have a most difficult job. The hours are long and the pay is woefully lacking."

Wanda and Jasmin departed, closing the door behind them. The judge was quiet for several moments. He rubbed his age-spotted hands together. "Miss Strickland, off the record, did you feel there was a rush to judgement in this case? And were you pressured by Charlie Rinds' political power?"

She looked at the judge and shook her head in tiny shakes. The case that began as a potential career maker now seemed like a curse. She was tired, which made her answer tersely, "The more I dug into the case the more I began to have doubts. Mr. Rind kept calling the office and demanding justice. When I didn't move fast enough, he called my boss, who called me. So, yes, lots of pressure."

"I appreciate your honesty. Court will resume in fifteen minutes."

Alex and I walked in the direction of the courtroom, while Wylene excused herself, and told us she would meet us in the courtroom.

***

We were back at the defense table. Wylene whispered something in Alex's ear and then patted my arm and smiled as if she knew secrets that I was not yet privy too. Alex merely nodded confidently.

The judge entered and sat. "I understand that the defense has one more witness."

Alex rose and said, "Yes, Your Honor. We would like to call David Wade to the stand."

"Any objections, Miss Strickland?"

She rose quickly. "None, Your Honor."

"Swear him in," the judge stated.

Alex didn't really question his witness as much as he simply asked him to tell his story. David did so calmly and without emotion. He spoke of the abuse suffered under the hand of Althea Rind and while he could not state that every foster child had been abused by her. He knew, because he saw it firsthand that all the children that lived there during his ten years were verbally and physically abused. He pointed to a small scar beneath his right ear. "She swung a wire coat hanger at my back and I ducked. This is a reminder of that."

"Why didn't any of you come forth with this information before?" Alex inquired.

He shook his head and breathed heavily. "Shame. Our backgrounds. Who would believe us? And the gift money at Christmas encouraged us all to remain silent."

"Why are you here today?" Alex asked.

"Someone showed up at my door and was quite convincing that it was time to do the right thing." He pursed his lips. "Past time," he added.

Alex sat down, and as he did so, A.D.A. Strickland rose. The judge smiled at her. "One moment please." She sat back down.

The judge looked to David. "Was Mr. Rind involved in any of the physical abuse?"

"No. He was genuinely concerned for our welfare. She made such a big fuss of wanting to be the one to take care of us and he was gone so much, and when he was home, she put on an act of Godliness."

The judge nodded several times. "Questions, Miss Strickland?"

"No questions, Your Honor. I would like to make a motion."

The judge's hands were loosely steepled. He opened them and gestured for her to continue.

"Dismissal of all charges."

"I could not agree more. Motion granted. Mr. Hurley, you're free to go." There was an immediate roar from the courtroom. The judge banged the gavel three times and silence ensued. "On a personal note, to all of you men that showed up today to support your old coach. I have seen a lot of character witnesses in my time on the bench, that quite frankly, I questioned the sincerity of most of the time. But all of you, showing up, ready to post everything you own to free your coach. I have never witnessed anything like it. I know your coach surely is touched but this old judge has been as well. I once played baseball. I was nothing special as a player. I played second base for a man named Ed Wilson. He had a great influence on me. He's in his nineties and living in an assisted living facility near here. I believe I'll visit him this weekend and tell him all the lessons of life he once taught me. This session of court is over and you men are free to greet your coach."

***

Teke

I had received a text from Bret that all charges were dismissed. I was not surprised as I had been praying all morning and I felt a certain peace that everything would be okay and that Clint would be coming home. I suppose that is why I am already sitting in my SUV, parked outside the courthouse with a very special passenger. I watched as people began to file out of the courthouse. There was a swarm of news media set up waiting for Clint Hurley to emerge.

171

I smiled and rubbed Josie's head. She was more alert than she had been in days. I had the leash in one hand and I opened the door. I stepped out and I was attempting to clip the leash to her collar when I heard the roar of the crowd. It startled me so much that my attention was diverted temporarily, and in that moment, Josie was out of the car and racing toward the front steps of the courthouse. I ran behind her, calling loudly, but Josie charged ahead, running up the twenty-four steps that led to the landing area outside the courthouse doors.

Josie began to work her way through the crowd. She bumped a few legs to persuade people to move. I lost sight of her in the crowd but I could hear her loud shrill bark.

I saw Clint, Alex and Wylene stand proudly, a few feet from the first step, basking in the sunshine of a cold winter day. The three of them with their arms linked around each other. They looked so triumphant.

I saw my husband hug Alex fiercely and then ruffle his hair like he was still his ten year-old little brother. I was almost to them now but I didn't see Josie. Frantically, I looked around. I heard that shrill bark again and this time her master had noticed as well.

I observed him as he searched the crowd and I knew the moment when he saw her moving among the legs of the people. He sat just above the first step and waited. Josie was all over him in an instant. She rubbed against him, whined, and backed away only to do it again and again. It was if she was trying to get so close that she was inside of him but she already was. She finally settled on to his lap and pressed her head into his chest and finally was still. He buried his head in her smooth coat. That photo was on the front page of *USA Today* the following morning. But even better, a local reporter had seen Josie escape from me and began filming. The video went viral. There were twenty million views of it by the end of the next day. Josie was a rock star.

I clicked the leash to her collar. "This dog is way too smart for me," I exclaimed.

Bret and Alex held a hand out to help Clint to his feet. I gave him the lead. "When's the victory party? We can have it our house," I said.

Clint smiled wearily. I could see in his face the toll of the past few days. "I want to go home. Can we do it tomorrow at my house? I am hoping that Wanda is bringing Jasmin home later today and I want some time with her and Josie. It appears my parenting days are not over."

"That's right," I said.

"I'll need some help," he replied.

"Just try to raise that little girl without us," Bret interjected.

"I wouldn't and I couldn't."

Bret turned to Alex. "Can you stay through the weekend and hang out with your brother for a couple of more days?"

"I can manage that but I have a request. Pig picking for the celebration."

"I can do that." He paused and turned to Wylene. "Miss fashion model, do you have any clothes for a pig picking?"

"Lest you forget-I'm a southern girl. I grew up in Kenansville. This ain't my first rodeo or pig picking."

There was laugher all around as Wylene strutted down the steps. The crowd parted as if they were part of the red sea.

Fourteen
Clint

Josie and I rode home with Bret. He had not spoken since we picked up my items from the jail. I was glad to leave behind my jumpsuit that was such a hideous shade of orange that not even a fanatical Clemson Tigers football fan would wear it. Josie was stretched out on the seat between us and her head was buried into my abdomen as I rubbed her head gently. I silently thanked God that we were together once again. We need each other. That much is a certainty. I felt her shudder a few times and her back legs began to twitch. She let out a couple of muffled yelps.

I looked over at Bret, who was smiling in my direction. "I think she has finally relaxed. She has not slept well since you were taken from her. We did the best we could."

"I know."

Bret reached over and rubbed her back. "She is an amazing dog."

"Do you think I have to worry about animal control coming for her?"

"No. Wylene got to the bottom of that as well. It turns out there was not a mark on the detective. Josie never penetrated the clothing. Plus the detective was wearing a tactical vest. It was needed for a dangerous criminal such as yourself." We shared a soft laugh together as we rode in the tranquility that the country offered.

Bret drove on to the dead-end road that led home. "Let me out here. I want to walk the rest of the way."

Bret pulled off on to the shoulder of the road. We got out and leaned against the front of the truck. I held Josie on lead. A fleeting lone cloud temporarily obstructed the sun but it was quickly gone and the warmth of the sun on this glorious cold day returned.

"How do I say thanks? What words would suffice for all that your family has done for me?"

Bret shook his head. "There's no need."

There was silence and I knew that there was nothing I could do that would make this right. Maybe sometimes, you just have to accept people's help. As I looked to the sun, I saw a red-tailed hawk flying low. I wondered if my Allie was looking down. Some would say with a certainty she was but we can't know any of this for certain while we are separated from what lies beyond the cobalt colored sky I'm gazing at.

I thought of our last moments together and what she said to me. "Look for the angel." My angel was a lost, frightened, abused little girl and if God had brought me through these arduous circumstances than I'll trust him that she will be with me. I'll watch over and protect her with each remaining breath I'm allotted and I'll place what she needs above my sorrow at missing the larger part of my heart. Maybe Allie is privy to my new outlook and if that's the case, she's smiling.

"Do you really not mind that we have a pig picking at your house? Killing the fatted calf and all?"

"I think it's good and right to celebrate this. Besides, how much fun will Jasmin have?"

"She's a special girl," Bret said.

"Indeed, she is," I agreed.

"I'll be over early tomorrow morning and I'll begin to teach that little girl the art of cooking a pig."

"You have done it often?"

"I have watched it done often." He smiled. "Teke's dad, Clarence, cooked a pig every Christmas and about every Thanksgiving until he passed away. I couldn't cook one this Christmas. I was caught up too much in what was lost. He was the dad that I never had and without question the finest, most decent man I have ever known, but I'm so blessed. I still have Teke, my children, grandchildren, Alex and good friends. I'm even making new friends." He paused, before continuing, "I don't know if I could continue on without Teke and I can only imagine your grief but I believe God is opening the doors to help you with this final chapter of your life. I find that it's usually God when it makes no sense to us or the rest of the world. He seems to take great pleasure in that. Confounding the so called wise of this world and us at the same time.

He smiled at me in such a manner that it led me to believe that he possessed additional information that I was not yet privy too. I looked at him and narrowed my eyes but he simply continued smiling. We turned to each other and shook hands firmly and held that grip for several moments. "See you in the morning," he said. He got in his truck and drove away.

I began the walk home. I neared Lori's house and I turned back to make sure no cars were on the road. I unhooked Josie. "Scout, girl." She trotted ahead and stopped every few feet to make sure I was still with her.

As fate would have it, Lori was walking to check the mail. She appeared to be lost in deep thought and Josie startled her by trotting to her. She saw me and astonishment consumed her face. Maybe she thought I had escaped the hoosegow and she was at grave risk.

"Hi, Lori."

"Hello,' she said, softly, dropping her head, failing to look me in my eyes.

"It will all come out that the charges have been dropped. I didn't want you to be nervous about living down the road from such a hardened criminal."

"I know. I saw it on the news. I'm so very sorry that I doubted you. You'll discover that I made some horrible allegations on television."

"I know. There was a television in the county jail."

She dropped her head in shame.

"I forgive you. We are neighbors and I don't want this lingering over us."

"That's far more gracious than I deserve."

"It's over as far I'm concerned. My not wanting to be involved with you had nothing to do with you. I had my one true love for a long time. Anybody would be a very distant second place to my Allie and I'll not cheat anyone that way. No one should be a consolation prize."

"What can I do to make up for what I have done?"

Her face was consumed with sorrow and I felt sympathetic toward her. I smiled and offered, "Nothing. It's over. I'm a man of my word."

She nodded her head gently and a few tears escaped and she wiped them away and turned abruptly, walking hastily back to her house. The mail apparently could wait.

As we drew near the cabin, there was a car in the driveway that I didn't recognize. A man stood and his two small boys stood with him and then he began to run to me and I started to run as well or more likely, I trotted only slightly faster than my current walking pace.

We stopped as we reached each other. I waited for my son, Dylan, to speak. His face was troubled and his eyes clouded in pain. "I don't deserve your forgiveness for what I have done."

"Shh," I responded, and I pulled my little boy in close and held him tightly, as he wept on my shoulder.

"Can you?" he asked.

"I already have."

He shook his head, not understanding. But what I knew is my son had come home. It was a time for grace. I looked behind him and saw James and Eric standing on the porch. I motioned for them to join us and they took off running as hard as they could. I bent down to greet them and James reached me first and almost knocked me over. I wouldn't have cared. Eric was right behind him and they

177

hugged me fiercely. Josie, not wanting to be left out of the group hug, barked and began to wiggle between us all. I felt my son's arms around me. All that I had been through the past few days was worth it for this one precious moment.

"Is anybody hungry?" I asked.

The boys shouted, "Yes."

"Let's go home."

The boys trotted ahead and Josie ran with them, barking excitedly. I looked at the cabin that was a dream of Allie and mine. It had been a building before without her but I realized in this moment it really was home. Home until my Father brought me to my final destination.

I thought of Bret's strange words. Kill the fatted calf and I laughed at what he already knew. My prodigal son had come home. I hope the Lord will be okay that in lieu of the fatted calf we will be dining on pig instead. I felt my son's arm around my shoulder and I smiled and looked to the heavens and winked. Maybe she was watching.

We were all on the porch. Josie barked at me and trotted toward the woods that led to the river. She had missed our routine. I smiled and asked, "How about a little stroll before I cook us a late breakfast?"

All three of them nodded and Dylan said, "Sure, Dad. Whatever you want."

The boys ran to Josie and we walked behind them. All was quiet, save a few birds singing to each other. My eyes were drawn to a massive Laurel Oak tree and I saw that Red-Tailed Hawk again. Oh, it could be a different one but somehow, I knew better. We had reached the bench now and Eric asked, "Why is this bench here in the middle of the woods?"

"I read here sometimes or I sit and watch Josie enjoy the smells of the forest." I pointed to the firepit. "Sometimes, I even have a fire."

It was James now. "Can we do that sometime?"

"Of course."

"When do you have to go home?" I asked, turning to my son.

"I'm not sure that we are," he whispered. "Lot to talk about Dad."

"I got time."

"Is this where you were when you saw the little girl?" he asked.

"Yes."

"Amazing." He smiled at me and asked, "Do you think the courts will allow you to have her?"

"I think so. She's a very bright, mature little girl and she will be quite adamant as to where she wants to be."

"Maybe, I can help," he suggested.

"How is that?"

"We're not returning to Columbia."

I waited for him to continue. He looked at the boys running toward the river and he started to call to them and I said, "Don't worry. Josie will not allow them to get in trouble. She will herd their butts right back to us."

He smiled and nodded. "Later, I'll tell you the entire story. But right now, I just want to rest with you. Help you, if I can."

There was silence and we looked through the trees toward the river. We watched as a large bizarre looking bird flew above us. The bird, the likes of which I have never seen, had a uniquely shaped bill. The body was bright pink, the legs more of a ruby red color and its tail appeared to be orange. The bird was flying south with purpose.

"Roseate Spoonbill."

I looked at him curiously.

"Strange." He paused before continuing, "They are not known to fly much farther north than Charleston if I remember correctly. I saw lots of them in Texas on my trips there. I guess the bird is lost and out of place." He waited a few moments before adding, "Just like me."

I shook my head and said, "No, Son. You're home."

He nodded gently his appreciation at my words but I knew he was astray for now and it would take time, but just as the bird was flying south to where it belonged he had driven north to a safe place that would help him sort out the misdirection of his life.

"How is your brother?" I asked.

"Why did I look up to him so much when you were the role model I should have been following?"

I shook my head. "When you boys were growing up it was not a bad thing but then—"

"Money and things became his God and I followed right into that deep pit. People always say money does not make you happy but we chase it at the expense of those we love just the same. I haven't been happy in a long time."

"Your journey is not over," I offered.

He nodded ever so slightly to me and then turned his attention back toward the river, where we could hear the faint sound of the voices of happy children.

We heard Josie's shrill bark. I recalled soon after we got her that I read something about how their bark could be so shrill that it can set your teeth on edge. It was true, especially when she was a puppy. I suspected the boys had got a little too close to the edge of the bluff for her liking.

"Should we check on them?" he asked.

Before I could answer Josie was herding the boys back to us. They were running and giggling as she kept barking at them and bumping the back of their legs.

"Time for breakfast," I said. The boys and Josie trotted ahead and I walked with my son in the quiet harmony of the forest. There was the distant tapping sound of a woodpecker's beak against a tree.

"Dad, can the boys and I stay for a few days while I sort things out?"

"You take my room. I rarely sleep in the bed anyway."

"Dad."

"Don't argue with me."

"Do you think Jasmin will mind that we are here?"

I shook my head.

He looked around as if searching the woods for the misplaced parts of his life. "Quiet and peaceful here. Columbia is so big and it seems that it's never without sound."

We were at the cabin now and I unlocked the door and the boys ran in excitedly. They ran up the stairs and Eric shouted down to his dad. "Can we sleep up here?"

"Better ask the owner."

"I built it in hopes that you would."

"Dad, I have a lot of money," Dylan offered.

I said nothing.

"I'm not bragging."

I waited for him to continue.

"If you have internet, I can manage my properties from here and I'm not traveling to buy any more, at least for now. I just want to take care of my boys and spend time with you." He paused before adding with a trailing voice, "Lost time."

My phone vibrated in my pocket. It was Wylene. I looked at my son and he nodded and said, "Take the call, Dad. I'm not going anywhere."

The call ended and he asked, "Any problems with Jasmin?"

"Not really. Wylene said there was a little hang up with the paper work and everyone is signing off for her to live here, at least temporarily, until the court decides for the long term. She assured me that she will personally deliver her to me early in the morning."

"I would like to help," he offered.

"I don't need money."

"What I mean is this. Jasmin wants to live with you and you want her. The one thing the social services and courts are going to be concerned about is your age. That's where I step in and say in the case that anything happens to you before she's an adult. I'll step in and take over."

James leans over the rail and shouts, "This place is so cool."

His dad nods gently in his direction.

"Son, don't make any rash decisions right now. There's time."

"Dad, I believe I'm seeing things much clearer than I have in a long time." He paused, before adding, "How much land do you have?"

"Five acres."

"Would you sell me one acre?" He continued without waiting for my answer. "I was thinking that the boys and I would like to move closer to you and just to be clear I'm not talking about building any mansion. I'm going to give the one in Columbia to Tara. It's paid for and she can sell it and have all the money. In keeping with the conformity of your land, I was thinking we could build a log cabin."

"We?" I asked.

"Think you're up to it? I was told that's what you did with this one. We could do it together. Sub contract parts of it but do as much of it as we can. Hire some local help you may know."

"One dollar."

"Excuse me, Dad."

"That's my asking price for the acre."

"Sounds fair. Can we build it close to the river?"

"The river bends a bit behind us and there's a good high place where you can build. It sure would provide a place to see beautiful sunsets. "How big of a log cabin?"

"Bigger than this but nothing massive. I want simple. Four bedrooms. A room for the boys and one for Jasmin, in case she wants to spend the night."

"That sounds reasonable."

"I have one more request before we shake on this."

I shook my head in feigned dismay. "No wonder you're rich. You drive a hard bargain."

"A concrete pad for a basketball court. My boys love basketball and who knows maybe Jasmin will want to play as well."

"Okay, but you're paying for that."

He laughed and stuck out his hand. I clasped it firmly.

It was late in the evening and James and Eric were sound asleep upstairs. My son and I sat by the fireplace enjoying the warmth of the fire. Josie was curled up close to it with a watchful eye on me.

"Still adhering to mom's rule of no more than two drinks in one day?"

"Yes."

"Do you think we could have one tonight?" he asked.

"Sure. Crown and a splash of ginger ale?"

"Sounds good."

I went into the kitchen and removed two Old Fashioned glasses from the cabinet. I smiled as I thought of a little prank to play on my son. I made the two drinks and then I removed a large cup that held about a quart of liquid. I filled it up with ice and nothing else. I hid it behind me. I gave Dylan his drink.

"Where is yours?"

I produced the quart size cup and rattled the ice in it. He looked at me perplexed.

"She limited me to two drinks a day but she didn't specify the size of the cup." And then as I observed the startled look on my son's face, I began to laugh. And then he joined my laughter that continued for several minutes. It was one of those wonderful times when you think the laughter is over and then you look at each other and it begins anew. I walked back to the kitchen and dumped the ice into the sink and retrieved my drink. We touched glasses and I said, "Welcome home, Son. Welcome home."

As we nursed our drink, silence ensued and I knew my son was trying to find a place to begin where he could tell of the events that led him to my door. He studied the fire intently as I was but I snuck a few glances his way. His expression never changed and if he noticed me looking his way, he failed to acknowledge that. Maybe I could help.

"How did Bret know that you were going to be here when I got home from the courthouse?"

He was silent and one thing I noticed was he didn't ask, "Bret, who?"

Finally, he said, "He told you."

"No, but he used the term kill the fatted calf. I didn't know what he meant at the time."

He nodded lightly. "He called the day you were arrested. I have no idea how he obtained my cell number. I told him I didn't want to come; He said he hoped I could live with myself, and that it wouldn't be easy." Breathing deeply and sighing, Dylan continued, "His call unsettled me and it made me think of how l had left my boys the day after Christmas for a business trip. I decided to come home early from my trip. That's when I discovered Tara in our bed with one of the Pastors from our church."

He shrugged and said, "I never had a clue. That's what I get for staying on the road so much."

Knowing that a mega church the size of the one he attended had many pastors on staff, I asked, "The senior pastor?"

Shaking his head, he said, "No. It was Pastor Harper. He performs the nuts and bolts type stuff so the senior pastor's time can be better spent elsewhere. He's the one that disciplines or even fires staff if they get out of line." He chuckled without humor as he added, "Earlier this year he fired the assistant worship leader because he was living with his fiancé."

I turned and looked at him with a startled expression. "Yes, he was sleeping with my wife at the time."

"Talk about a log in your own eye," I interjected.

There was silence again for several minutes and I noticed his glass was empty as mine was. I took his and moved to the kitchen to make another for each of us. I grabbed the quart cup and held it up. "Dylan, you sure you don't want me to make you one in the big cup?"

He smiled through his pain. "Thanks for making me laugh."

"That was laughter?"

"Laughter will return, Dad. Probably sooner than you might expect." I waited for him to elaborate. "You can't walk into your house and find your wife in bed with another man and not be stunned, but I am seeing things in a new light." He fell silent again. He drank from his glass and then continued. "None of this is a surprise to you as I always knew you didn't approve of my choice of a wife, even though you never said anything derogatory about her. But I loved her intelligence, her beauty, her always rock-hard body, the way men looked at her and then at me because she was my wife. I thought we would be such a good team. But I don't know if I ever truly loved her. It was more of an image of what we were together. I think I made another business decision when I married her and I believe she did likewise."

"Did you confront him?"

"You mean did I slug him like you did Wade?" He didn't wait for an answer as he continued, "I asked Tara where the boys were. They were next door at the neighbor's house. She was yet another member of our church who knew of the ongoing affair. I turned to leave and retrieve my boys. Harper suggested that we keep this quiet for the sake of the church. I stepped into the hall and then the business side of my brain kicked in. I heard movement behind me and I pulled my phone out, touched the camera icon, stepped back into the room as they both were standing naked with their clothes in hand. I snapped a few shots. Talk about a deer in the headlight expression. They couldn't speak, so I did. 'In case, you fine

Christians try to deny this later, I'll always have this leverage. Tara, you can have this home to sell, your car and all your possessions. That will leave you well off financially but that offer will end if you do not grant me full custody of my sons. I won't stop you from spending time with them. I'll be fair but I'm leaving the area and they are going with me and hopefully it's not too late to teach them all of what is really important in life, because all of this stuff," I said, as I motioned with my hand. "Well, it's just stuff."

He sipped his drink and rattled the ice in it slightly. "That's the story. I had a long talk with the boys on the way here. I turned off my phone and they put away their tablets and we talked without interruption. They told me Pastor Harper came by often when I was away. James was curious enough and at that inquisitive age where I believe he was putting things together and of course he told his little brother."

"What about your brother?" I asked.

"He wanted me to keep it quiet. Harper's family is quite wealthy and they live in the Charleston area. Wade has some big money leveraged with Harper's family on a joint venture and that was his greater concern. I spent my life following his lead, seeking his approval, but never again. He never showed an ounce of concern for me. Not once did he ask how I was. He asked me where I was going and I said home to help our dad and he should do likewise. He cursed me and called me a fool."

He lifted his glass and swirled the amber colored liquid. "Dad, thank you for your grace and forgiveness. I hope I'm wrong but I don't think that things with Wade will ever change. In his mind, everything is your fault and now all of what has transpired will be my fault." He began to chuckle. "I forgot one part of the bedroom scene. Harper asked me if I found this to be terribly upsetting because he was black. I just shook my head and answered, "I'm pretty certain that regardless of race I would not be happy to come home and find my wife in bed with another man.

"I took one call from Tara after we left. She said that Harper and she were in love, and she really wanted a life with him. She would sign the papers and not fight for custody of the boys. It feels like I won. I just hope the boys will be okay in the long run."

"They will." He looked at me and I nodded firmly. "They will."

"And you'll help."

"I'll help and you'll help me raise a little girl. Neither of us has any experience in that area but thankfully for us she's much brighter than you or I."

"I love you, Dad."

"I love you, Son, so much so that I can't express it."

He laid down on the couch and closed his eyes and in just a few moments I heard a slight snore. I covered him with a blanket and kissed the top of his head like I had done a million times when he was little. I smiled and I noticed how peaceful he looked and I thought of the courage he had displayed by baring his pride and coming to me.

There was a faint knock on the door and I possessed no inkling of who might knock on my door at this late hour. I walked to the door and Josie went with me. I opened the door and saw Wanda Thomas. The lady from Social Services. I instructed Josie to stay as I stepped outside.

"I'm so sorry to come here so late but that's one head strong child," she said with a shake of her head. "She refused to sleep one more night away from her home. I could get in all sorts of trouble so this never happened." She turned in the direction of her car and motioned. The door opened and Jasmin stepped out and smiled as bright as any of the stars in the sky on this clear winter night. Then she took off running and I stooped down and she leapt into my arms. I heard Josie pawing at the door and I asked Miss Wanda to please open the door.

Josie was whining and trying to wiggle between us. Jasmin giggled and said, "Stop it, Josie."

Josie went behind her and stuck her head between Jasmin's legs. Jasmin was still hugging my neck tightly but then she lessoned her grip and pulled away. "You still want me, don't you?" She was grinning from ear to ear and she knew my answer. She had found a safe haven from the storms of this life, of which she had suffered so many, at such a tender age. She was home. I looked up into the night sky and whispered, "Thank you, God."

I heard a sniffle and I looked at Wanda. She was wiping tears away. "I have to be tough and I can't allow myself to get emotionally caught up in my job or I won't do it well. And I don't see that many happy endings. I'll do everything I can to make sure she stays with you. Now, I'm going home."

"Thank you, Miss Wanda," Jasmin said sweetly.

Her stern face was back. She pointed her finger at Jasmin and squinted her eyes. "You better listen to Mr. Hurley."

Jasmin smiled broadly as Wanda walked to her car. "Wanda," I called out. "We are having a celebration pig picking tomorrow. Please come."

She turned back and was in thought as to her answer.

"Please, Miss Wanda," Jasmin said. "You can make sure that I'm behaving."

"I do need to check on your welfare."

"Food will probably be served around six," I said.

She nodded and walked to her car. Jasmin and I watched her drive away.

"My son and his two sons are here."

"I know. Miss Wanda told me."

"She did?"

"Teke and Linda watched his boys while he went to find David. The first person the Rind family ever adopted. He talked him into coming to court."

"But David doesn't live here," I said.

"He has family here that he just happened to be visiting."

I took that news in. My son had found a way to make the Rind family back off and he never said a word. "Wait a minute; how do you know all of this?"

"I might have eavesdropped on one of Miss Wanda's calls."

"Jasmin," I said with a shake of my head.

She grinned again and looked up at me with those dark eyes. "It was for the greater good."

I shook my head and laughed.

She said, "I have a question."

"Go ahead."

"What am I going to call you? It can't be Mr. Hurley and Clint doesn't sound right or maybe Mr. Clint wouldn't be so bad," she said as her voice trailed off.

"My grandsons call me Pop."

She deliberated for several moments. "Are they going to be around for a while?"

"It appears so," I answered.

"Are they nice?"

"Yes."

"Do you think they will like me?"

"I do."

"Okay, Pop."

I took hold of her little hand and we walked inside.

Fifteen
Clint

The light was dim the following morning when I walked outside with Josie. She ran around to the back of the house which was not her normal route. I smelled smoke in the air and I walked toward Josie to investigate.

"Sleeping on your shirttail this morning, are you?"

Bret was already set up with the pig cooker smoking and a roaring fire blazing in the portable fire pit nearby. Jake and Josie were sniffing each other excitedly and trotted off in the direction of the woods.

"I tried to be quiet but I was still surprised that I didn't wake you, backing the pig cooker up and setting everything up."

"Where is your truck?" I asked.

"Teke helped me set up and then drove back home to sleep. She isn't tough like me."

I laughed. "I'm pretty sure she's tougher than you."

He tilted his head to the side. "You don't say." He rubbed his whiskered face and added, "Actually she was up kind of late making slaw. My grandmother taught her how to do that. I'm surprised Josie didn't alert when we parked and started unloading things. She was probably just exhausted."

"I doubt it got past her. I would bet she knew who it was and just wanted to stay close to me."

"I don't doubt that." He paused before asking, "How do you feel?"

"Hopeful."

"That's a good place to be." He paused and adjusted his worn black ball cap. There was a logo of a hand saw and hammer crossing each other diagonally. The word, Marin was on top of the logo and below it read builders. "You had a late-night visitor," he said.

"I guess Wylene spread the news."

"She called Alex last night."

I walked over to the pig cooker and placed my hands on the handle.

"Do not even think about lifting that and interfering with my heat." Suitably admonished, I lifted my hands and backed away.

"I brought this portable fire pit to keep warm but I thought later this afternoon when guests begin to arrive, we would have a fire out front as well. It's not supposed to climb out of the forties today."

"That sounds like a good idea," I said.

"You think a man can get a cup of coffee around here? My travel mug was empty an hour ago."

"You bet. I will have one with you. I'll be back in a few minutes."

The dogs returned and Jake plopped down by his feet. Josie was by my side.

Returning, I gave him his coffee and pulled up a chair beside him. Josie laid down next to Jake. We sipped our coffee in silence for several moments. "My son is here and my grandsons."

"I suspected as much."

"Kill the fatted calf," I said, turning to him.

He nodded with a smile.

"We stayed up late talking like we have not done in forever. He has had a hard blow but I think he will be just fine. In fact, I think because of this he will be better."

"Have you processed that maybe he might not have come here right away if not for you being arrested?"

"Romans 8:28, huh? *And we know that in all things God works for the good of those who love him, who have been called according to his purpose.* I have to admit I have struggled with that one a time or two."

"I have as well." He drank from his coffee cup, before adding, "Dylan wanted to be one of those ball players that stood up in court for you since he played for you as well but I think he didn't feel worthy for that but what he did do was so much more important. Finding David Wade and persuading him to come to court."

There was silence for a few minutes before I offered, "Probably just be a few of us this afternoon and evening."

He shook his head. "I think every ball player that stood up yesterday that's in town will be here. Adrian wanted to stay but he said he had to get back to Raleigh and sell some cars to take care of his family. He also pulled out his phone and showed me pictures of his beautiful little girl. He is one proud daddy." He paused, before adding, "Pretty strong statement when your rivals show up to help."

"Very humbling," I offered.

"I didn't have a high school coach like you. You taught them far more than basketball and that's what a really good coach does."

Everyone from inside came out together. Jasmin hugged Bret's neck and asked him if Miss Teke was coming over later.

"You bet. Maybe now that all of you are awake, I might be able to get some breakfast."

I rose but I felt my son's hand on my shoulder. "Dad, let me do it. You stay in the chair and enjoy your day."

"I'll help," Jasmin said.

"We will too," the boys said together.

I nodded my head. "Thank you. Jasmin knows where everything is."

The door closed behind them and I smiled at how full the cabin was. "Dylan is moving here with the boys."

Bret studied me and waited for more. "But not his wife." He sipped his coffee and waited for me to continue.

"I know I can't ever repay you. You brought your brother here and he made everything happen." I guess I have no shame because I had more favors to ask of a man that I owe such an inordinate debt.

"Are you going to ask me or not?"

"My son wants to build a home here. He wants a log cabin, somewhat like mine but big enough to accommodate two growing boys and Jasmin, in case I'm not here to see her to adulthood. He was looking at some plans on his laptop. Maybe, you could look at them."

"I would be glad too," he answered.

I hesitated.

"And?" Bret added with a smile.

"He has plenty of money but he wants us to build it. He's going to take a break from actively working and live on his investments." I was struggling to ask my real favor, when Bret said, "Do you mind if I help you guys out? That would be fun to build a log cabin from start to finish."

I shook my head at his offer, as he continued, "He has two boys, so we need to start soon. Allow me to act as contractor and I'll take care of all the permits. It will be faster if I do it."

I nodded my appreciation. "I hope I can hire Foster again and if Trey is available, him as well. I'll just have to make sure my son, knows not to pay Foster one dollar above whatever they agree on. I learned the hard way. Maybe Trey won't be so full of himself this time. Are you sure Teke won't mind?"

"Not at all. In fact, you know she will want to help as well." He was silent for a few moments. "I have a suggestion, actually it's from Teke. It's about Jasmin."

"What?"

"Teke said with all Jasmin has been through it might be best if she homeschools hers for the remainder of this school year."

"I think that's wise and I'll talk to Jasmin about it but I'm sure she would be good with being taught by Miss Teke.

"The kids want a basketball court. I'm sure you know someone Dylan can hire."

"I believe in my limited conversations with Foster that he's pretty good at that and I know my way around a little concrete work myself. What if we let the kids help? It will make them appreciate that court all the more."

"Great idea," I readily agreed.

***

It was past four and the skies had turned gray. The sunlight we had enjoyed this day, faded to obscurity. Bret was in the back and beginning to pull the pork apart. I was building a fire in the portable fire pit that I brought from Carolina Beach. It was one of Allie and my favorite quiet times.

The house was full of helpers. Teke, Alex and Linda, had arrived at noon. Teke had brought chicken that had been marinating all morning in George's Barbeque Sauce. Bret cooked the chicken on the pig cooker. Linda whipped up a garlic potato dish to go with it and it was as fine a lunch as I have enjoyed in quite some time.

Linda and Teke had planned on cooking and cleaning but the children insisted on taking care of the cleaning chores. The way Jasmin took charge, my guess is she was behind that. The boys seem to follow her lead without dispute.

Teke and Jasmin talked about homeschool and Jasmin was excited about it. They both agreed that she would attend public school after the summer break.

The fire was burning well now and I sat in a chair and reflected on the past few days. Bret startled me from my thoughts. He handed me a paper plate with ribs and a paper towel. "Appetizer," he said.

I took one bite and said, "Wow. I think Clarence would be proud."

He smiled and gently nodded his head. "Good fire," he said, warming his hands over it. "You were pretty deep in thought. You want help building something else?"

"I wasn't thinking about that, but now that you mention it. Since it's no longer only me, I probably need some storage."

"We could do that in conjunction with the basketball court. Build an oversized garage."

I hadn't heard the quiet footsteps of my son. "That's a good idea, Dad. Why don't we build one big enough for all of us?"

"If you think that you can afford it," I added, with a chuckle.

"Do you think that we can all go to church Sunday?"

"I don't see why not," I answered. I felt his grip on my shoulder and then he walked back inside.

"Back to the cooker," Bret said as he walked away.

A black Volvo SUV entered the driveway and I blinked twice to make sure my eyes were not failing me when the driver emerged. Charlie Rind walked toward me, appearing hesitant, not at all like the self-assured representative on television.

I stood uncertain of what his intentions were. I heard light footsteps behind me and I felt a small hand clasp mine. "I'm not going back with you," Jasmin stated fiercely.

He held his hands up. "I mean no harm."

I felt a presence on my other side and I knew that it was my son. We all three stood in awkward silence. Charlie Rind looked lost and unsure. His world had been turned upside down. He rubbed his white hair and shook his head. "So weary, but I'm sure it's nothing like the hell you have been put through and even more so for you, Jasmin." He stopped speaking and it became eerily quiet.

"It's my fault," he finally offered. His body wavered as if some unforeseen blast of wind had knocked him off balance.

I motioned for him to sit in the chair across from me. "Maybe we could all sit," he suggested.

My son pulled two more chairs up and the four of us sat near the fire. It was quiet and only the sound of the fire was heard for several moments.

Charlie rubbed his hand through his hair. "I'm sorry, Jasmin. That's not enough for what you have been through. My not knowing is no excuse. I hope that in time you can forgive me. After court yesterday, I called every one of the foster children that ever lived with us. Some of them cursed me. None forgave me. I don't blame them. I don't blame you if you can't forgive me. My soon to be ex-wife was escorted off in handcuffs an hour ago. She will receive no aid from me."

I turned to my son. "Please take Jasmin inside."

He looked at me intently and I nodded softly. "Okay, Jasmin, let's go inside and help," he said.

She was slow to rise but she did as she was asked and I waited until I heard the door close.

"Congressman, you—"

"Charlie," he said softly.

"Okay, Charlie, you never knew those children were being abused?"

He dropped his head in shame and then he shook it. He rubbed his forehead. "Lord, I need a drink."

"You got the first three words of that sentence correct," I replied quickly.

He looked at me with puzzled expression and then he thought about his words. "Lord, I need…" and his voice trailed off. "Too late for someone like me, way too late."

"That is not true. We can all be redeemed."

"I wish I could believe that," he answered and then he closed his eyes and his head dropped and for a moment, I thought maybe he had drifted off to sleep. "I was in D.C. so much and I left the children to her. I never saw anything when I was home to make me suspicious. I'm not here to offer excuses. I have none, Mr. Hurley.

None. I'm sorry for what I put you through. These past days have been a nightmare for you." He sighed and tapped his chest. "My fault. All my fault."

"A nightmare for you as well, Charlie."

"But I deserved mine."

I wanted to tell him he was wrong but I could not find the words at that moment. Maybe I just did not have sufficient grace.

"Jasmin wants to be with you and she deserves to pick her family. I'll not contest it any shape or form, and Althea is not going to be in any position to be heard."

"Do you think she will go to prison?" I asked.

"It depends on how many of the kids come forth to testify. If they all do, I don't see any way she avoids some serious jail time. She blamed me for being gone. I'm here, apologetic and guilty but I never hit one of those kids ever. It's important to me that you believe that."

"Jasmin said you never touched her and she never saw you strike any of the other children."

"I'm still guilty."

I could not disagree with him.

Another car was driving in and Charlie Rind rose slowly as I did. "Enjoy your evening. Please forgive my intrusion but I had to at the very least look you in the eye and apologize."

I extended my hand and his face tightened in surprise. He took my hand and shook it firmly. "God bless you, Sir."

"And you as well," I replied.

"I'm pretty sure I don't deserve his blessings."

"None of us do, Charlie."

He studied me and didn't respond.

"What will you do?" I asked.

"I don't know where to begin."

"The truth is always the best place."

"In politics that's always the last resort and even then, never divulge it all." He chuckled and shook his head. "My dad is long gone but when I first told him many years ago that I wanted to be a politician, he said, 'Why not a more honorable profession, like say, prostitution?' I tell that as a loosening up joke when I speak to folks but the truth is my dad was serious. I'm glad he's not here. He would be ashamed of what I have become. I went to D.C. with such aspirations, but you keep selling little pieces of your soul until you have nothing left. You lose the ability to see anything in black and white. It's all colored in a thousand shades of gray."

"I'm just an ordinary man but I watch famous people get in trouble and they lie and then they allow one layer of the onion to be peeled away. But then something else comes out and it's another layer, and so the process continues. If they would just come clean all at once. We are a forgiving people for the most part," I offered.

"Rip the band aid off with one good yank?" Charlie asked.

"Exactly."

"I don't have much to lose, do I? I was going to run one more time and that was it. There's a national wildlife bill that I'm working on and I really want to see it to fruition. But I have to win one more race and this one has suddenly become far more difficult than I anticipated."

"Tell the truth," I repeated.

He nodded and I wondered if he would. "You're no ordinary man, Mr. Hurley. Those people that stood up for you in the courtroom. I was certain that you had hurt Jasmin but listening to those men gave me great pause. I'm very glad that Jasmin found a place of safety with you." He walked away without another word. It seemed as if he had aged a decade since I saw him in court.

I heard two doors open at once. The car door of the person that had driven up while Charlie Rind was departing and the front door to the cabin. Josie was quickly by my side.

As the man approached, I noticed that he was dressed in khaki pants and wearing a black law enforcement jacket. The sight of any law enforcement at the moment made me fear the worst. Josie stepped in front of me and began growing very low and very intently. It was then that I put it together. This was one of the detectives who knocked me down and handcuffed me.

He stopped at the sound of her growl. He was fifteen feet from me. "I came to apologize," he offered.

I placed my hand with my palm down. "Josie." She did as I commanded but continued to growl. "Settle," I said and she was silent.

"Am I safe?" he asked.

"She has nipped one person in her life and she won't leave my side unless I tell her she can. Sit in the chair," I said, pointing at the chair that Charlie Rind had just vacated."

He adjusted his belt that held all those law enforcement gadgets and sat. His eyes remain fixed on Josie.

He shook his head. "The entire time we were here that morning, I knew something was not right. I tried to tell my partner but he was so gung ho. It was Congressman Rind's child and he wanted to be a star. I don't blame your dog for protecting the little girl. The entire situation was out of hand. I'm glad the truth came out and I'm here to say, I'm sorry. I'm glad that your dog is okay. I'll gladly pay the vet bills out of my pocket."

"She's fine. We don't need anything from you."

He nodded his head with understanding. "I wish you well. I understand the little girl wants to live with you and I hope it all works out."

I looked at Josie and she had her head placed between her front paws and while she was still looking intently at him, I could feel her mood soften.

"That's all I have. I would shake your hand but I'm not sure she would allow that and I doubt that you would want to anyway. I can't blame you."

"Porch," I said, firmly. Josie looked at me and hesitated. "Porch," I repeated, and this time she ran several feet before bounding up the six steps to the porch. She sat on the porch, continuing to observe.

I rose from my chair as he did and extended my hand. He shook it securely. "Nick Smith, Mr. Hurley, and I wish you well."

"Thank you for coming by, Nick."

He nodded and walked away. As he drove away there were three cars coming in my direction. There was scarcely any light left, save the glow from the fire. I walked to the porch and petted Josie. Two surprise guests back to back and I was about to be surprised by a third. Lori stepped out of her vehicle and opened the back door, gathering what appeared to be several large same size plastic containers. I walked to her and she held them out to me. I took them and I could smell a plethora of different cookies.

"I saw the pig cooker go by my house early this morning. I was having trouble sleeping due to a guilty conscious. I assumed that there was a celebration planned so I baked cookies. My peace offering. There's oatmeal, pecan, chocolate chip, and walnut. Forgive me for tooting my own horn but I am a fairly good baker. You and your guests enjoy these and I'll leave you to your party."

"Why don't you stay?" I suggested.

She shook her head quickly. "No. Everyone here will hate me and I don't blame them." She wiped the tears that seemed to form in an instant.

"I told you that it was over. Forgiveness is whole and resolute or it's not really forgiveness."

I heard footsteps behind me. It was Teke.

Lori looked at her embarrassed. "I did that dreadful interview and I castigated a fine and decent man for no reason other than my own pettiness. My own foolish wounded pride."

The car behind Lori belonged to Wylene. "Bob is out of town but I'm here," she announced, with a beaming grin. She was wearing black jeans, gold cowboy boots, a black shirt peeked out in places not covered by her denim jacket, and to top it all off, she wore a black Stetson cowboy hat. I chuckled at her outfit and how I had learned in a very short time that style and elegance wore on her as comfortably as a thick down comforter on a cold winter night.

"You're blocked in now. You might as well stay," I offered to Lori.

"I can't. I'm a horrible person. No one will want me here."

"Not true," Wylene generously intervened. "You just made a bad mistake and that in of itself does not make you a bad person. And I love your outfit. Come with me. Let's see if we might rustle us up a glass of wine out here in the wilderness."

Lori surrendered as everyone seemed to do in the presence of Wylene. Wylene kissed my cheek and Teke led the two of them inside.

It was as if the dinner bell had sounded all at once. The cars rolled in. I stood by the fire and greeted many of my former ball players. Wanda walked to me with a huge smile and hugged me. "Invite a southern girl to a pig picking. I might report this as an attempted bribe of a social worker. I could smell it time I got out of the car. Where is the food?"

I laughed and pointed her inside.

Foster and his wife, Carol arrived next. "I heard a rumor that we have another log cabin to build."

"Are you in?"

He smiled his boyish grin, hugged me and said, "What do you think, though I heard your son was rich so I'll need a pay raise this time."

"I'm sure we can work something out."

Kim and her husband, Gary were next. "I brought deviled eggs," she said, motioning toward the large glass plate Gary was holding.

"Thank you." I pointed to the Fosters. "Follow them."

Kim hugged me and said, "I'm so happy that little child is going to be with you."

"Thank you for all that you have done."

"You can bring her by my shop now anytime. We have to fix her up right now that she's here for good. What I don't have we can order."

"Please charge someone this time," Gary said, in a dry southern tone.

She turned to her husband. "You hush your mouth, right now." Turning back to me, she said, "He doesn't mean it. He just likes to talk tough. He knows where his bread gets buttered," she said, with a wink and an ever so sly smile.

**

It was past ten o'clock and the crowd had thinned during the last hour. I am pretty certain that no one went away hungry. I was enjoying the fire and the company of those around me. I was surrounded by Dylan, Alex, Linda, Bret and Teke. The children were inside watching an ACC basketball game.

We all had a mug of hot chocolate and we were passing the cookies around and kept debating as to which flavor was the best. I went with the pecan but they were all delicious and I should know because in my festive mood I tried them all.

The door opened and Wylene and Lori emerged. Wylene, the tough protector of her clients and friends had offered such soft charity to Lori. Lori had loosened up and began to enjoy herself. Perhaps the wine had aided the cause.

They hugged each of us good bye and walked to their cars. I overheard Wylene say, "Darling, I have just the man for you to meet. Yes, I do." They giggled like school girls.

The kids came out and Jasmin said, "We are going to bed now. I'll make sure they brush their teeth."

We all chuckled as they took turns hugging us. Jasmin came to me last. She hugged my neck and said, "I love you, Papa."

"I love you," I replied.

"The boys can call you, Pop. I decided that I like Papa better."

I nodded in agreement.

We sat there, without words. There was a glow that went beyond the fire that roared in the center of us. I reflected on all God had done. I could hear my wife saying, "If God brings you to it. He will bring you through it." I'm seventy-three years old and I have another child to raise. My son is home, along with my two grandsons. Life could never be what it was with my Allie but I'm surrounded with family and friends. We have a log cabin to build. And while I'm certain I'm somewhat partial—I have the greatest dog in the world.

I hear the door open. "Papa."

I turned toward the door to see Jasmin in dark blue pajamas. "Josie is whimpering for you."

"Come," I shouted. She ran to me and jumped into my lap and settled into a tight little ball, keeping a keen eye on the fire.

I rubbed her head and pulled on her ears gently as I thought back to all that had transpired since Christmas Day.

I was ever so grateful for the girl in the river, my angel.

Epilogue
Jasmin
(Thirteen years later, September 14)

I'm typing away on my lap top, telling the story of a young girl who was once rescued by an old man and a dog. The two of them still walk in the woods nearly every morning but it takes them longer to reach the bluff that grants them an unobstructed view of the river and then to return home these days. Papa is eighty-six and Josie, sixteen. She's more content these days to heel by his side than to run ahead exploring. I worry about them walking in the woods at this stage of their lives, but at the same time I know without question that it's not something to be taken from them.

We could tell Josie's hearing was weakening the past couple of years. The Vet confirmed our suspicions that she was almost completely deaf. Papa took it in stride and purchased a vibrating E-Collar. As it was with all things, Josie figured out what to do right away. I have observed often, Papa rub her and say, "I love you, Josie." And though she can't hear his words or his tone she looks at him adoringly with her fading amber eyes when he says it. I don't know what to make of this other than Josie must see the love in Papa's eyes. Who knows? I would not put it past her to have learned somehow to read lips.

Josie has always been so attached to Papa but even more so the last couple of years. Even when Papa takes a shower, she follows him to the bathroom, where she sits patiently and waits for him to pull the curtain back and reemerge. I think she's keenly aware that the light in each of them is waning with each passing day. Papa has heart problems, and I have noticed his breathing of late is often quite labored. I struggle to see him as old. This is a man that I watched build two log cabins when he was in his seventies. He split wood right up until the past fall, when his grandsons begged him to let them take over the chore. He sadly relinquished that duty.

I'm a recent graduate of UNC-Wilmington and my first real job will be as a legal secretary for Auntie Wylene, who is in her early seventies, and still practicing law with the same fervor as when she went to bat for me long ago. She still turns heads and ignites a spark to any room she enters. She knows what I really want to do is write, but you have to pay the bills along the way. Besides, like she said, a few years of working in the legal system will grant me a lifetime of stories.

My creative writing professor emailed a literary agent he knows who is quite interested in my so called, fictional story. An old adage is that truth is stranger than fiction and if you doubt it, you need only to consider my story. An abused orphan takes off in a kayak on a snowy, frigid, Christmas day, and … well you know the story. It's difficult to believe, yet I have lived it.

They did indeed build a log cabin for Dylan and my brothers that was completed by the end of that summer, along with a basketball court and an oversized garage. We all played basketball the right way, taught by Papa. He attended every home game and more times than not, he and Dylan attended away games. I think they enjoyed the rides, and welcomed it as a time for the two of them to catch up on the seasons of this life they missed out on.

James and Eric played on the varsity boys' team and I played on the girls during our sophomore, junior and senior seasons. During their senior year both of my brothers made the third team for the eastern region. I made first team.

The boys also attended UNC-Wilmington, even though Dylan had enough money to send them anywhere. The boys never said so and neither did I, but when it was time to choose a college, I believe we all wanted to hang on to our time with family for as long as God allows.

As our interest in basketball grew, there was an added perk. Teke's brother, Money, would provide all of us tickets for Portland's games versus Charlotte each year and sometimes we went to Atlanta, when they played the Hawks. Dylan would hire a company with a big van to drive us. That way we could all enjoy our time together and not worry about driving or parking. Money retired three years ago but he can still get us tickets when Portland comes to our state, but Papa has more trouble with the travel these days. He tells us to go without him but it would not be the same. Besides, I would worry about Josie and him being here alone.

We all have done well in school and anytime we struggled we simply called Teke. She always made time for us. I have watched and admired Bret and her love story continue, even as they are now in their seventies. We all celebrated their fiftieth wedding anniversary a few years ago. Alex's gift to them was a trip to Alaska.

The respect, the admiration, the gleam in their eye for each other has not diminished with the seasons of their life, even now as they have transitioned gracefully into the winter of their story. I rarely date as I have been so focused on school and starting my career, and taking care of Papa. But when that time comes, I know what to look for, thanks to the two of them. I'll settle for nothing less than love that treasures each tender moment.

The second summer of our life together was spent in Lansing, North Carolina. Papa found a way to try to repay Alex. Papa, Bret, Teke, Foster, Trey, Dylan, the boys and I all worked to build the log cabin that Alex and Linda desired. We all lived together in the overly spacious house that Alex and Linda lived in at the time. They desired a simpler life as their kids were transitioning into their own lives. It was not long after taking Papa's case that Alex sold his practice to his partner, for a fair price, just as his predecessor had done for him. He still worked out of the practice when he occasionally took a case that intrigued him. Maybe he kept an iron in the legal fire in case one of us was to get in trouble as Papa did so many years ago.

During construction of the log cabin, Foster drove home every weekend because he said his wife, Carol, had attended church without him for far too many years when he was in the military. Trey rode with him each weekend and often stayed at their home. They became the parents that Trey never had.

Charlie Rind, believe it or not went on national television the morning after he apologized to us, and he stood there without flinching or making excuses under the bright lights of news cameras and persistent questions. As I heard, Pastor Jeff, once say, "An, 'I'm sorry, but…', is no apology at all." I wrote Mr. Rind one Christmas and told him that I forgave him. I had no desire to see him again but I think that's understandable. It's a part of my life best treated like the wake behind a boat. I don't regret that time because it helped shape me into the strong woman that I am. Besides, when you consider my early years with my mom and then the subsequent years with Papa and this wonderful family, except for that tough middle stretch, I enjoyed a pretty good childhood.

Charlie also won his next election in a landslide and then true to his word he retired when his term was up. A politician being truthful. As Papa said, "Who ever heard of such a thing?"

Dylan's ex-wife, Tara, married the pastor she had the affair with. There were photos on the church website. Wade was one of the groomsmen. They divorced within three years when she arrived home to discover him in bed with a young college girl. As usual Papa got it right: "Building a house correctly means beginning with the proper foundation."

Dylan's children are my brothers in every way but blood. We would all fight to the death if someone attacked one of us. When we returned from the mountains during the year that we built Alex and Linda's cabin, just before Labor Day, Dylan met Tina, a lady at the church we attend with Papa. She grew up in the country and she cherished country life. More importantly, she loved Dylan, for who he was. He never had that before. James and Eric saw their mother occasionally when her busy schedule permitted it. This past year she married husband number four or maybe it's five. It's difficult to keep track of. She invited her sons to fly to the Bahamas for the wedding. I couldn't help but laugh when Eric looked at his brother and said, "Let's skip this one. We can always catch the next one."

Dylan and Tina married the summer after they met. She was never able to conceive but she looked upon my brothers as her own children. In some ways, it may appear that we all lost a lot of our family, but we gained family not by blood, but by choice. I think each of us has emerged all the richer.

Wade has never made an overture toward Papa or Dylan. Papa sent a Christmas Card with a personal note each year and each year they were returned unopened.

I rose from writing and walked to the corner of the living room. I throw the switch on the transformer and watch the old trains roll through. Papa shared the story of how this was his last Christmas present from his wife. I doubt she had any inkling that Papa would have so much help putting the train set together. We all helped with the project but the most enthusiastic participant was Dylan. Papa stepped back and allowed him to lead the project. I would observe Papa sometimes and see this contented smile as he watched his son become a child again.

The snow-covered landscape has trees, caves, and the various wildlife that resides in Alaska. It's a beautiful layout and Papa has said often that he could never have made it look so spectacular without us.

I find it ironic that Papa regularly talks about how much we have given to him, when we all know that he's the cornerstone of this family. I know that he's sad that he will probably leave this world without reconciling with Wade but because of the past and the divide and hurt that occurred—all of that made Dylan and his relationship stronger and closer than it could have ever been otherwise. I can tell Dylan still feels guilt occasionally for times lost, but a better more faithful son you'll not find.

I turn the trains off and walk outside on the porch. The heat of summer has subsided somewhat but the sweltering humidity remains. It hasn't rained in the last week or so and the many Japanese Maples now bordering the cabin at the edge of the woods need watering. Papa, Dylan, my brothers and I had planted each one of them.

We thinned areas to allow them room to grow. Papa said it was best that they enjoyed filtered light and not the scorching direct sun of summer. Last year they gave off a pretty dazzling array of Fall color. We are hoping for an equally impressive display again this year but if it remains this dry it's rather doubtful that the color of last Fall will be rivaled.

Next month is Papa's favorite month. He loves the Fall when the air cools and the humidity lowers. I feel sadness as I know that he does not have many Octobers remaining.

I touched my afro that I have kept since Miss Kim did it long ago, and in fact, she still styles my hair to this day. She sold her shop long ago and Gary and she retired to their farmhouse, where I visit and get my hair did as we girls say in the south. One potential boyfriend suggested I change my hair style. He was gone shortly after that remark. Maybe I should alter it and perhaps my reasoning for not doing so is silly. That time Miss Kim changed my hairstyle to an afro and Papa met me in that church parking lot. I saw something in his face. His concern, and even though I was only ten years-old at the time, I knew I was safe with him. But more than that, I believe that was the very moment Papa fell in love with a little girl. My afro reminds me of that time and besides I look pretty darn hot with it. Papa taught me among many things that I was beautiful, and I didn't need to chase every fashion trend that emerged but to just do what I think is best regardless of what is in vogue.

I look at my watch and debate about venturing out to check on Papa and Josie. It's not as if these walks have not been without incident. Five years ago, Papa had a heart attack, right in front of the spot where they saved me. Josie knew right away something was amiss. She wanted to love on him and she kept putting her head under his chin and nuzzling him. Papa told me later that he managed to grab her face firmly with one hand, and he said as sternly as he could muster, "Find Jasmin."

We used to play games in the woods and it was Josie's favorite. She knew everyone's name and we would hide behind a tree and someone would say, "Find Jasmin, or find James or Eric." She would take off running until she found us. She loved that game and all of us did as well. On that terrible day, however, it was no game. I was inside the cabin when I heard scratching on the door. I opened it and saw only Josie. I knew right away something was amiss. "Find Papa," I said, and I took off sprinting behind her.

Papa was in the hospital for four days. It probably would have proved longer if not for a very wise humble heart doctor. Dr. Nicky Pipkin was in his early sixties. He casually carried a youthful smile that permeated kindness. The second day that Papa was in the hospital, he asked me into his office to inquire about Papa's home life. He listened intently and his eyebrows arched when I told him about the bond between Josie and Papa.

He thought for several moments and then he reached for the phone on his desk and placed a call. "Can you please come to my office?" he asked

Minutes later a security guard entered. He was probably near fifty years of age. He was fit, with broad shoulders, a boyish face and light brown hair. He wore rounded spectacles encased in a silver frame.

"What can I do for you, Dr. Pipkin?" he asked.

"Jasmin Hurley, this is Jack Humphrey. He is in charge of the security for the second shift. Jack, I need your help. Her papa had a heart attack and we need to lift his spirits.

"Thirty minutes after visiting hours are over tonight. I want you to meet Jasmin at the private security entrance. You can show her where when we finish here."

"I don't understand," I said.

He laughed for a moment and then said, "I get lost in my own head sometimes and forget to distribute my plan of treatment. I want you to bring Josie. Don't tell anyone, including your Papa."

Josie is...," Jack asked gently.

"An Australian Cattle Dog," Dr. Pipkin answered.

"Well, this is a first," Jack said.

Dr. Pipkin turned to me. "I will be waiting for you in Mr. Hurley's room tonight."

That night Jack led Josie and me to Papa's room. Josie began whimpering before Jack opened the door.

"Josie," I heard Papa say with increased strength in his voice.

She jumped up on the bed and laid her head gently under Papa's neck. He was home two days later.

I smile at the warm memory of that night a doctor prescribed a dog for his patient. Standing on the porch, at that instant, a forlorn feeling sweeps over me that reminds me of the sentiment I feel late in the evening, on Christmas. My favorite month and my favorite day, but I'm always so sad to see it depart.

I hear the sudden shrill bark of a cattle dog. It's a sound I hadn't heard in quite some time. Something is wrong. I race back inside the cabin, grab my phone, and the pistol that Bret had taught me how to use.

I sprint through the woods. My heart pounds so loudly that I could I feel it in my ears. I hear Papa yelling, "Go away! Get back!"

I run past the fire pit in the direction of the sounds. I hear Josie yelp and I run faster, my heart racing, my lungs gasping for air. I round the last turn and see three large coyotes surrounding Papa and Josie, who was bloodied, but standing her ground fiercely in front of Papa. I must act fast because Papa is dangerously close to the edge of the bluff. One coyote has blood dripping from his mouth as he attacks Josie again. That one yelps once and falls limp, as Josie manages to tear out part of his throat. I raise my gun to fire in the air and scare the rest away. Before I can one of the other coyotes charges at Papa who lands a stiff kick, but in the process, steps backward and disappears over the ledge. That coyote turns towards me and I drop him with one shot. The remaining coyote runs away and I race to the path that leads to the shore of the river. I'm already crying when I make it to Papa. Blood streams from his mouth. I sit down, cradling his head in my lap. "Oh, Papa."

He shakes his head ever so slightly and manages a weak smile. "None of that, child. We had a good run, you and I." He lifts a hand and touches my hair. "I love you, Jasmin."

He gazes behind me toward Josie. She can barely walk but she limps toward us, collapsing on top of his chest. He strokes the side of her face like I watched him do a million times. I don't know when I have observed a greater love than this wonderful dog has demonstrated to my Papa.

He whispers, "Please don't allow her to suffer."

I looked at the carnage of her injuries. One side of her is almost completely torn out. I place my head on her body. "You dear sweet, wonderful girl."

I call 911 and give them directions, but I know there is no need to hurry. I call Teke next and explain the help I need.

Josie refuses to move and maybe she has no energy left to even lift her head. "You did good," I hear him say. There was a rattle in his voice. Our time together is close to an end.

"It all makes sense now," I hear him say, as he struggles to breathe. "I dreamed last night of rolling green hills and magnificent skies. Allie and I were holding hands, running, and laughing. We looked like we did when we first married. Josie ran with us, barking joyously. The rainbow bridge is real. I hate to leave you but God is calling me home to my baby."

"Thank you for saving me," I said, as I sobbed. He coughed up blood and I tilted his head slightly. I wiped the blood off with my shirt sleeve.

His voice temporarily gained grit as he gazed into my eyes. "You saved us that day. You brought my son home and my grandsons. I gained a wonderful daughter-in-law. You did all that Jasmin, my marvelous girl in the river. I love you sweet child of mine." He coughs up more blood. I wiped his mouth again. He smiles and says, "It's time for me to go. God is calling me to join my baby."

Those were his last words spoken on this earth. Josie, sensing the life leave him, started to squirm into him as she often did. I feel a part of my heart evaporate into the heavens and I know he is gone. She raises her head and looks at me with the most heart wrenching countenance I have ever witnessed.

"He's gone, girl," I say, as I gently rub her head. She laid her head back down across him, her neck once again, meshed with his.

I hear faint sirens in the distance, growing louder. Josie is still breathing, but just barely. She whimpers softly periodically.

The sirens grow louder and I soon heard voices from above. The first responders were here. I gently rubbed her head and wished that she was gone but she continues to breathe. She whimpers once again and it sounds like the cry that I have heard hundreds of times, when she was dreaming.

I am stiff from holding Papa's head in my lap. They are here now. I hear them speaking but I have no idea what they are saying. I ask for the foam headrest on the gurney. A pleasant looking Hispanic man, not much older than me, with dark hair, a well-groomed beard, and kind eyes, gives it to me. I slide it under Papa's head as I tried to move away and stand. The same rescue man offered both of his hands and helped me up.

"He's gone," I say.

He moves to check his pulse and to my shock Josie turned and nipped at him. He backs away as she growls lowly. There are four rescue personnel and they all stand unsure of what to do. Each time one of them tries to talk soothingly to her and approach Papa. She bares her teeth and growls.

The four of them talk among themselves. I see Bret and Dr. Lanier arrive, the same vet who protected Josie many years ago.

Dr. Lanier moves in close and is also greeted by a menacing growl. She shakes her head also unsure of what to do.

"He said; don't let her suffer before he left." I shake my head and bend down beside her again and rub her head "She killed one coyote. He was her world. She loved us all but…" I say, my voice trailing off like a vapor disappearing into the air.

"Josie," Bret says as he kneels down. "Good girl," he says softly. Josie looks at him and then turns back to Papa and licks his face several times. She whimpers softly for several moments. The EMT who helped me up, wiped his tears away.

"You have pentobarbital in your bag?" Bret asks, looking up at Dr. Lanier.

"Yes."

"Only one way to do this," he said as he looked at me and nodded.

I sighed heavily and said, "Walk me through it, Doc."

I listen and did as instructed. Josie doesn't resist my efforts. As I injected her, I thought of Papa's dream and I said, "Today, you'll be with him in Paradise." Moments later I feel her life depart.

***

It's was eight days later, on the first day of Fall, when we gathered behind Dylan's house, overlooking the river. Alex had read the instructions Papa had requested in his will that was revised, soon after he took me in. I did take one step that was not included in his directions, as we didn't know that Josie and he would die minutes apart from each other. They were both cremated and I had their ashes placed together in a temporary urn.

Until Papa's death, only Alex knew that he had brought Allie's ashes here and scattered them in this very spot the year he was building his cabin. That's why he suggested Dylan build here.

Papa told Dylan and me last year that he wanted his funeral to be private and brief and he made us promise. Still, we heard from many of his ball players and several of the people he attended church with. The condolence cards would arrive daily for six weeks. There was even one from Charlie Rind.

The evening of the incident, I received a phone call from Papa's friend, Bryan, in Ohio. We didn't need to call anyone because the story of Papa and Josie was on the national news. The old dog that rallied one last time in her long life to fight for who she loved the most. The old man who went to his demise, literally kicking, as he fought off a coyote.

I thanked Bryan for giving Papa Josie so many years ago. I told him that not only would Papa not have lived so long, but that I would in all likelihood not be here.

There was silence on the other end of the line and I thought that the call had dropped but his wife had taken the phone. "Bryan can't talk any more. He walked outside. After all these years, he still thinks he has to hide when he sheds tears, which is very seldom. He loved your Papa greatly and he's grateful that he could have a part in Josie and him being together for all these years. He said it had to be God for the two of them to die within minutes of each other."

In attendance, that morning of vivid sunshine, and a few stray clouds, was a small intimate gathering. Bret, Teke, Alex, Linda, Dylan, Tina, and my brothers. Our minister, Pastor Jeff, led the service.

I saw Bret Marin try to speak but after saying, "I'll miss you my friend," he broke, and Teke had to take over.

Dylan told a few stories about Papa and Josie. My favorite one was about the night that we had the pig picking to celebrate my new home and Papa being set free. He, Papa and Josie sat alone by the fire for one hour after everyone left. Later when everyone was in bed and Josie was in the recliner with Papa, settling in to sleep, she did a peculiar thing. She got up from Papa's chest, jumped down and looked at him. He thought maybe she had to go outside to potty but when he walked to the door, she didn't move. As I have heard Papa often say, in a somewhat bewildered tone, "What, girl? I don't understand."

She walked to my bedroom door, sat and stared intently at the doorknob, waiting patiently for him to open the door. Papa thought that perhaps she wanted to sleep with me. He opened the door and she walked to the bed where I was sleeping and studied me for several moments as Papa observed. Next, she turned around and walked out as Papa closed my door. She walked up the steps, leading to the loft. Papa was curious by now and he walked with her. She went to each of the boys' beds and took a turn looking attentively at each of them, before turning back to Papa and walking down the stairs. She then went to Papa's bedroom, where Dylan was sleeping. Papa tapped on the door and Dylan told him to come in. He was in bed and when Papa opened the door, Josie walked to him, sat by his bed and looked up at him. He rubbed her head and looked with a perplexed expression at Papa.

"I think I understand," Papa said. "Go to sleep. I'll explain in the morning."

Papa went back to his recliner and Josie climbed in after him. She nestled her chin under his. Papa rubbed her and said softly, "You just had to check on all your cows, huh girl? Everyone is safe. You can rest now."

She continued to do this each night and most of the time we were all asleep and never knew that we were her last chore of the day. After Dylan and my brothers moved into their new home and it was only me to check on, some nights I tried to stay awake until I could sense her, sitting by my bed, staring at me in the darkness. On those occasions I would whisper to her, "Thank you for checking on me, Josie."

It was my turn to speak. I had no tears left and I could not find sadness knowing how happy that he was to be reunited with Allie. I also knew that Josie was surely with him and I don't know that either one of them could have lived without the other.

"I'll repay your love and kindness that you gave so freely by doing my best to make you proud." Then I added, "Was that short enough?"

There was laughter among us all. We took turns scattering his ashes. Pastor Jeff closed us with prayer and one of Papa's favorite scriptures, Psalm 91:1. *He who dwells in the shelter of the most high, will abide in the shadow of the Almighty.*

We all walked toward the cabin that I would continue to live in when I heard Dylan say, "This can't be good."

I looked at the man charging toward us and I knew without question that it was his brother, Wade. He stopped in front of us and stared at his brother. "Where is the will?"

"Really?" Dylan asked. "You refuse to speak to him and you think you deserve something?"

"Mom would want it that way," he replied with a snort.

"Not with your behavior, she wouldn't."

"So, you get it all?"

Dylan smiled and said, "No. There's a binding will and on the top of that will, Dad wrote. The little girl gets it all."

"That's correct," Alex stated. "I'm his attorney and I assure you this will is ironclad."

Wade looked at me in disbelief. "She's not even his child."

"Oh, I think Dad would disagree with that. She's certainly proven more his child than an ingrate like you," Dylan responded.

Wade was in front of Dylan now. Their faces inches apart. He placed a hand on Dylan's chest. "I want my half."

"It would be best if you removed your hand," Dylan said firmly.

"Like you're going to do something, little brother," he said derisively.

There was no flower bed to catch Wade this time. He fell on the gravel driveway. Courtesy of a short right punch from Dylan.

Pastor Jeff shook his head and walked toward his truck.

We walked away without a thought as to Wade's well-being, though I suspect as it was once before, that it's his ego that's bruised the most.

Dylan said, "I don't know if Pastor Jeff will choose to conduct any more funeral services for the Hurley family."

We all laughed together.

"Well, is the little girl throwing us out?" Dylan asked, with a smile. "He never did put the land in my name."

I smiled back at the man who paid for my education and so much more. Placing my arm around him as we walked, I returned his glowing smile and said, "No. We are family."

"We indeed are that. Every single one of us here," he responded.

In the days and weeks to come our family didn't mourn the loss of Clint Hurley, though we did miss him greatly. We spent our time being grateful for his being home with his Allie and how he had so greatly enriched our lives.

And we told stories that would be passed on throughout generations of the wonderous, courageous, loving, cattle dog that was Josie.

COMING SOON FROM MOONSHINE COVE

BILLY BEASLEY'S NEXT NOVEL

HOME

READ THE FIRST CHAPTER
BEGINNING
ON THE NEXT PAGE.

The initial morning rays of the sun flicker inside my bedroom, stirring me gently awake. Hesitantly, I reach across the bed, finding the presence of no one. She has departed, and for that, I am more than grateful.

I stretch my long body across the entire bed, enjoying the freedom, if not the overabundance of perfume that was left behind on the linens. I glance at the clock on the nightstand. There are two additional hours of sleep awaiting me. I smile lazily and return quickly to a deep slumber.

Within minutes I'm dreaming. It is one of those dreams that never make sense. There is a constant revolving of characters. I recognize some of the people, while others I'm certain that I have never laid eyes upon. That proves a mystery to me. How do people you don't know intrude into your dreams?

The wonderfully poignant song, *Late for the Sky,* by Jackson Browne, joins my dream. It takes me several moments to realize that it is not part of my dream but rather the ring tone on my cell phone.

The owner of the boat dock, Howard, my employer, is in Greece on vacation, so I rule him out. He is having too much fun with his tall, thin, blonde, mistress, who is probably half his age. That leaves only two other people that have access to my phone number and one of them just left. It has to be Jackson, my best friend, back in my hometown of Wilmington, North Carolina.

Leaning over the bed I reach for the black backpack on the floor. I pull the phone out and punch the button, feigning irritation. "Jackson, it is a little early."

"Trent, it's Linda." Linda is the youngest of my three older sisters.

"Daddy is dying."

My first thought is to say something clever like, "You have pronounced him dead for years," but I refrain. There is something in

220

her tone that tells me that this might not be the best time for my particular brand of wit. My family never understood my humor, but then they never understood anything about the wayward last child of the Mullins family. It proves easier, I suspect in many families, to place inaccurate labels on family members and never remove them. To eradicate those labels would be to admit you are wrong. Starting at the top with my father, admitting wrong is not something that exactly runs rampant through our family. I did not follow that trait from my father as I have spent most of my life trying to avoid being anything but him.

Don't get me wrong. I value his influence greatly. It is just that it came mostly in the negative form. I saw how he behaved. How he craved being the center of attention. How he could never really listen to anyone. He had two things on his mind. What he was saying and what he planned to share next. He could not acknowledge his many failings, so there was nothing to ever apologize for. I never heard the man say once, "I am sorry." And he had much to express regret for.

"How long does he have?" I ask.

"It's hard to tell."

"What does the doctor say?"

"Not a damn thing," she replies. There is a mixture of anger and sadness in her voice. I hear sniffling and I know that she is crying through her rage.

My father has lived with congestive heart failure for years. Countless times, and seemingly always in the dead of night, he has been rushed to the emergency room. Each time he survives much to the astonishment of the family.

She composes herself. "They just released him from the hospital after one week. The doctors told us the first day that he had pneumonia and today they discharged him and said basically nothing. If they sent him home to die, they could have at least told us."

"Maybe it is not that bad."

There is silence and I know that my response was not the correct one. That is to be expected. I am the baby brother of three older sisters-the only son of an overbearing father. It is a given that in this family I don't possess any accurate answers on this subject or any other for that matter.

"Well, why don't you remain in whatever hole you ran away to. You miserable bastard."

"That escalated rapidly," I say to an empty room, tossing my phone on the bed.

Linda could go weeks without cursing but when irritated she spews obscenity as gracefully as an inmate on a chain gang. She had just been adequately provoked.

I sit on the edge of the bed and contemplate my next move. I retrieve my phone and walk into the small kitchen and make a cup of coffee from the Keurig. I open the sliding glass door and walk out on to the deck. It is low tide and there is marsh grass, mud, and several pockets of water that have formed a rock's throw in front of me. Beyond the initial marsh grass, there is a narrow creek that eventually makes its way to and from the East River.

I drink from my coffee mug and breathe in the pungent odors of the landscape in front of me. Some people label the odor offensive but I am not to be counted in that group. The wind gently sways the plentiful grasses of the marsh. Directly in front of me, there are three great blue herons-to my left, in the distance, I see several snowy egrets. They are busy foraging the marsh as they often do at low tide. A Ring-billed gull is resting on an old round piling that holds a sign so rusted that I have never been able to read what is written on it. The gull seems uninterested in doing anything but observing.

Behind me, there is a small area of woods. The trees are mostly oak and they are kept in check with the salt spray. Most have crooked trunks and gnarled limbs. The underbrush is thick and only a fool would try to navigate through them. There is a lone dirt road through the woods leading to this place that I have resided, for right at two years. It is a small house, containing two bedrooms and one bath. It is less than eight hundred feet square feet and was built over one hundred years ago. It was obviously constructed well to have stood the test of the many storms that have battered the east coast.

The house rests on pilings on a tract of land that is twenty feet above the marsh. I was informed by the owner that the house had never flooded.

There are no neighbors and that works for me. It is quiet and peaceful and it has helped calm the demons that so viciously ravaged my mind not so long ago.

I call Jackson.

"Good morning sunshine," he answers. "Coming home?"

"See you this afternoon," I reply wearily.

"Your room will be ready," he states.

We hang up without saying good-bye.

I look around at the scenery and reflect as to the road that has brought me here too the coast of Georgia. I chuckle, as I recall the day that I sought out the owners of what would become my place of refuge.

I was kayaking, soon after moving here, and I saw the shack from the creek. I paddled up to the shoreline and pulled my kayak up on the beach. I walked around the structure and I saw no signs of anyone living there.

I was temporarily staying in a condo that Howard and his wife, Brenda owned. It was proving claustrophobic. I needed tranquility to mend the wounds that were razing my soul. I asked Howard about it and he just bellowed with laughter. "Son, you don't want to stay there. That shack is owned by the same black people that own the store in that community. Well, suffice to say if you drive through there you will be the only white face and you will not be welcomed."

I persisted, and he gave me directions to the store. The paved road turned to gravel and there was a weathered wooden sign, that read, *Dylan Town, Population-It Varies*. Behind the sign was a gigantic Live Oak tree that was at least sixty feet high, with a spread of over one hundred feet. Spanish moss clung to the branches. The first building was an old white clapboard church on the right. The grounds were well kept, and the church appeared as if it had just been painted. There was a steeple, with a large church bell residing below it. The homes were modest and well kept.

It was afternoon as I approached the entrance to the store. The wooden sign above the door had the words, Dylan's Grille, routed and burned into the wood. I took a deep breath and entered. Three older black gentlemen were sitting in brown, worn wood rockers in the corner, gathered around a large wooden spool, the color of an old barn. Two of the men studied the chessboard that rested between them. The other man was smoking a pipe and occasionally peering intently at the board and shaking his head as if he were privy to information the players were not. They all seem to notice me at the same time and in unison, they cocked their head to the left and constricted their faces in either amusement or astonishment. I can't speak as to which.

I heard conversation coming from the back of the store. I walked to the counter where a black man of impressive size, with a shaved head, was cleaning the grill. Beside him was a lady, I assumed to be his wife, wiping down the counter beside him. They were talking softly with each other. I cleared my throat and said, "Excuse me."

They both turned around. He tightened his eyes and she, though startled a bit, offered a smile. "Whatever it is we are not buying," he said firmly in a gravelly voice, before dismissing me as he turned back to the task at hand.

"I am not selling anything."

He started to speak and I observed the lady still him with a slight grip of her hand on top of his forearm. "What is it you want, honey?"

She was an attractive lady, medium height, and full-figured. Her eyes were wide and expressive and she reminded me of the actor, Alfre Woodard.

"The place through the woods. Do you rent it?" I asked, before interjecting, "I am sorry ma'am. I forgot my manners. My name is Trent Mullins."

She extended her hand. "Maybelle Dylan. That is Maybelle and not Mable," she stated firmly. "This is my husband, Moses." When Moses did not move fast enough to suit her, she stated firmly, "Shake his hand, Moses."

I am not a small man in any way but his hand engulfed mine with power and he held it a little longer than needed.

"Why would you want to live in that isolated old shack?" she asked.

"It's a long story, ma'am." She waited but I was not offering my narrative to anyone.

"Probably running from the law," Moses said under his breath, as he turned back to the grill.

She smacked him with her cleaning towel. He turned back around and narrowed his face. She placed her hands on her hips and raised her eyebrows at him as if he were a small child that needed reprimanding.

He glared at me intently and then he began counting off on his fingers. "No central heating and air. No air condition period. No cable. No phone. No WIFI. Power is about all you have and that is limited. You can't drink the water and you can barely stand to shower in it." He turned to Maybelle. "Did I leave anything out? Oh," he continued, "No white people."

I tried to suppress the smile that was fighting to escape. "Something funny?" he stated, not sharing in my amusement.

"Obviously, you sell things for a living and it appears to me you might be going about things the wrong way."

His eyes widened, and he was about to respond, but her hand was back on his arm as she snickered, and then laughed heartily. "Man got a point, Moses. Man, surely got a point indeed."